KILL AN INDIAN, START A WAR!

Comanche peace chief Ten Bears had come to Fort Sorrel to sign a treaty to bring a lasting peace to the Palo Duro country—but there were some white men who didn't want peace . . .

Waco looked next at the building. He discovered several men were standing just inside the main entrance. One of the group suddenly lurched through the batwing doors. Tall and lean, he was shaggy haired, unshaven, and wearing a low-hanging holster carrying a Colt Civilian Model Peacemaker. Teetering from the porch, he stared fixedly at the peace chief.

"That's the stinking son-of-a-bitch's killed my poor ole grandmomma!" the man bellowed. Reaching for the revolver, he went on, "And I'm going to pay him back for doing it right now!"

Even as the man commenced the draw, Waco was whipping his Winchester upwards . . .

J. T. EDSON'S
FLOATING OUTFIT
WESTERN ADVENTURES

J. T. EDSON'S
CIVIL WAR SERIES

OTHER BOOKS BY J. T. EDSON

J.T. Edson

OLE DEVIL'S HANDS AND FEET

They Were Called His Floating Outfit

CHARTER BOOKS, NEW YORK

This Charter book contains the complete
text of the original edition.
It has been completely reset in a typeface
designed for easy reading and was printed
from new film.

OLE DEVIL'S HANDS AND FEET
THEY WERE CALLED HIS FLOATING OUTFIT

A Charter Book/published by arrangement with
Transworld Publishers, Ltd.

PRINTING HISTORY
Corgi edition published 1983
Charter edition / August 1989

ISBN: 1-55773-232-9

Charter Books are published by The Berkley Publishing Group
200 Madison Avenue, New York, N.Y. 10016.
The name "CHARTER" and the "C" logo are trademarks belonging
to Charter Communications, Inc.

PRINTED IN THE UNITED STATES OF AMERICA

10 9 8 7 6 5 4 3 2 1

For Chris & Stewart Molloy, of the Sussex Punch, Milton Keynes, in spite of their Carvery having played havoc with my waist-line.

Author's note

As usual, for the benefit of new readers and to save our "old hands" from repetition, we have given details of the family backgrounds and special qualifications pertaining to the members of the floating outfit, also some of the points about which in the past we have most frequently received mail requesting information, in the form of Appendices.

We realize that, in our present "permissive" society, we could include the actual profanities used by various people who appear herein. However, we do not concede that a spurious pretense at creating "realism" is a valid reason to do so.

As we do not conform to the current "trendy" pandering to exponents of the metric system, we will continue to employ pounds, ounces, miles, yards, feet and inches where weights and distances are concerned unless we are referring to the calibres of such firearms as are already gauged in millimetres instead of fractions of an inch.

Part One, "Small Man From Polveroso City, Texas", appeared in the first issue of the regrettably short lived British *WESTERN* Magazine. We are grateful to the publishers for allowing it to be included in this volume for the benefit of those readers who have not yet seen it.

One version of *Part Two, "The Invisible Winchester",* was included in the first Wagon Wheel Western edition of *SAGEBRUSH SLEUTH,* but was subsequently deleted. However, we have been informed by Alvin Dustine "Cap" Fog that the source from which we produced this story was incorrect in some details. With his kind permission, we are now re-issuing it with the appropriate amendments.

J. T. EDSON,
Active Member, Western Writers of America,
Melton Mowbray,
Leics.,
England.

PART ONE

Small Man From Polveroso City, Texas

"What do you make of that, honey-bunch?" Margo Defayne inquired, frowning in puzzlement. "They're taking the *west*-bound train."

"They must have a buyer out West," Frederick "Honest Fred" Defayne replied. Then, seeing two men at the other end of the platform approaching the people to whom his wife had referred, he went on. "Only they might not get a chance to deliver. Could be this's the end of the line for the Duke and Duchess."

"It's what they deserve if it is, the 'mother-something' Limey bastards!"[1] asserted the buxom red head, her pretty —if too heavily made up—face and tone registering satisfaction mingled with righteous indignation. "Cutting the ground from under our feet like they did with the Zebra!"

Although the couple's accent was indicative of a less than affluent, and poorly educated upbringing in New England, their appearances implied they had now considerably improved their circumstances. However, as far as their choice of attire was concerned, coming into the possession of increased wealth had not been accompanied by the de-

1. See *Paragraph Two, Author's Note*. J.T.E.

velopment of what was accepted as good taste. They were dressed after the fashion much favoured by some members of the theatrical profession, albeit not those belonging to the higher echelons of the "legitimate" stage. Their clothes were rather more in the style of the kind who provided suitably gamey and unrefined entertainment in better class saloons, dance halls and beer gardens on both sides of the Mississippi River.

Of medium height and in her mid-thirties, Margo had on a purple dress which clashed with her fiery hair, but emphasized her Junoesque proportions, a feather boa and a large hat profusely decorated by artificial flowers. A few years older and bulky in build, her husband was clad in a pearl-grey derby hat, a loud check suit, a salmon pink shirt with an attachable white celluloid collar, a necktie of a hue which made the rest of his attire seem almost drab, and Hersome gaiter boots. Despite a heavy black moustache, his ruddy features suggested a jovial bonhomie. The expression was very much a part of his stock in trade, as was his wife's generally amiable expression, when they were engaged upon the various forms of illegal enterprises which formed their livelihood.

As was implied by the titles and derogatory comment uttered by the Defaynes with regards to their birthright the man and woman being discussed were British and, apparently, of a higher social status than the couple from New England. Also in their mid-thirties, exuding an aura of gentility, both were tall, slender, and by far the most elegantly clad of the people awaiting the arrival of the west-bound train at the railroad depot in Kansas City, Kansas.

Blonde, beautiful, if of an imperious demeanour, Sarah "Duchess" Grimston wore a well tailored black two-piece travelling costume, a plain white silk blouse and a Wave-lean hat. While simple in line, to eyes which could read the signs, the garments were made of expensive materials and her hands were concealed in a muff made from the skin of a sea otter. Also light haired and conveying a suggestion of aristocratic origins which accounted for their sobriquets, her husband, Albert "Duke", was dressed in a deerstalker hat, a tweed Norfolk jacket, corduroy trousers, calf high brown leather gaiters and untanned walking boots. He was carrying a brown leather portmanteau in his left hand and his right grasped a stout walking stick. As they were not accompanied by a porter, the former was apparently their only baggage.

Their appearance of gentility and elegance notwithstanding, the Grimstons were in much the same line of illicit business as the Defaynes. In fact, they had come to Kansas City with what had proved to be the same purpose in mind. However, judging from what the thwarted American couple could see, it seemed the English pair might have cause to regret the hitherto successful outcome of their illegal activities on the previous evening.

Defayne's remark about the possible fate of the Grimstons had been provoked by his identification of the two men, closely followed by a large sombrely dressed woman, who were walking purposefully towards them. The pair were detectives of the Kansas City Police Department. Despite his frequent disparaging comments regarding the intelligence of peace officers west of the Mississippi River, Honest Fred was willing to admit—albeit grudgingly—that they were as competent in their duties as any he had met in the East. Their presence at the railroad depot, accompanied by a woman he recognized as one of the matrons who dealt with female prisoners, had caused him to arrive at his conclusion. Out of consideration for his intentions where the English couple were concerned, he was waiting with mixed emotions to see what happened.

If the Grimstons were aware of the approaching trio's official status, they showed no sign of being alarmed by it.

For all that, the watching New Englanders suspected they might be equally well informed about the advancing threat. Either the sight of the detectives, or something else, caused Sarah to be so preoccupied she bumped into a passenger who was standing alone on the platform. Muttering what was probably an apology, she returned her right hand to the muff from which it had apparently been jolted by the impact. Having done so, she continued to walk with her husband until they were halted by the detectives. There was an overt display of badges of office and a brief conversation the Defaynes were too far away to hear, but could guess at what was being said. Then, having made what was clearly a protest and an explanation that they were meaning to leave on the west-bound train, the Britishers allowed themselves to be escorted to the building from which the peace officers had emerged.

"What do you reckon, honey-bunch?" Margo asked, after the party had disappeared.

"They don't have it with 'em," Defayne assessed.

"It looked that way," the red head admitted. "Or it could be they've got it so well hidden they're sure it won't be found."

"If it isn't found, they're going to wish they hadn't cut in on *our* game!" Defayne growled, then shrugged. "Anyways, there's nothing we can do except wait and see what happens."

Neither Margo nor Defayne had paid the slightest attention to the man with whom Sarah Grimston had collided. Apart from their desire to discover what fate had in store for the British couple, their disinterest where he was concerned was understandable. Despite the manner in which he was dressed, if it had not been for his momentary contact with the Duchess, they would not have thought him worth more than a cursory glance. From their point of view, nothing

about him suggested he might prove a suitable candidate
for their predatory intentions.

Not more than five foot six in height, giving the impression of being, at most, in his early twenties, the man's
tanned features were no more than moderately handsome
and far from eye-catching. A low crowned, wide brimmed,
black J.B. Stetson hat was tilted back to display recently
cut dusty blond hair. Knotted about his throat, the ends of a
tightly rolled scarlet silk bandana trailed down the front of
an open necked dark green shirt. Older than the rest of his
attire, the brown jacket he had on was somewhat baggy.
Hanging outside a pair of high heeled, sharp toed tan coloured boots, more suitable for riding than walking, the
legs of his new Levi's pants were turned up to form cuffs
almost three inches in depth. With the exception of the hat
and boots, his garments looked to have been purchased
recently. For all that, he contrived to give them the appearance of being somebody else's castoffs. In his right hand,
he held a small and battered portmanteau. However, although a person clad in such a fashion depicted in the periodicals of the day would have been illustrated sporting a
gunbelt with one, or two, revolvers in open topped holsters, he had no such gunbelt and gave no other indication
of being armed.

Such attire was common enough around those towns
further west in Kansas which served as shipping points on
the railroad for the numerous herds of half wild longhorn
cattle driven north from Texas. It was, in fact, practically,
de rigueur for the cowhands who brought them. However,
Kansas City was now only rarely visited by members of
that hard-riding, hard-working, hard-drinking and hard-
playing fraternity. Yet, for all the notoriety they had acquired as a result of the many lurid stories about their wild
behaviour when paid off at the end of a trail drive, this
particular denizen of the Lone Star State was of such a

diminutive and insignificant appearance, he went practically unnoticed by most of the people around him.

Most, but not all!

Three men standing just beyond the entrance to the platform were studying the small Texan with considerable interest. All were clad in the kind of suits, shirts, neckties and footwear worn by clerks, bank tellers, or office workers of other kinds. Tall, slim, good looking in a sullen fashion, two had a very strong family resemblance. Unlike their companion, who was several years older and wore a derby hat, they wore tan Stetsons with "Montana peak" crowns.

"Are you *sure* that's him?" demanded Rudolph Chufnell, looking past his slightly younger brother at the third member of their party.

"He's the only beefhead who's been to see Greenslade in weeks," Bertram Sutcliffe replied irritably, using the derogatory term for a Texan and having the kind of nature which resented any suggestion that his judgment could be in doubt. "And the old bastard had him in the private office as soon's the letter he'd brought was taken in."

"But we were told that Dusty Fog *himself* had been asked to fetch the documents!" Aaron Chufnell protested, his Mid-West tones expressing an equal irascibility. "Didn't you hear his name?"

"He never gave it," Sutcliffe answered sullenly, yet a trifle defensively. "All he did was give old Ramsgate the letter and said to tell Counsellor Greenslade's he comes from Polveroso City, Texas. But it was enough to get him fetched in straight away, so maybe he's Dusty Fog."

"*Him*?" Rudolph challenged derisively, jerking a thumb with obvious contempt in the direction of the man they were discussing. "Just take a look at him, god damn it!"

"Yes!" Aaron supported. "Even if only part of the things

you hear about Dusty Fog are true, could a short-grown son of a bitch like that be *him*?"

"You have heard about him, haven't you?" Rudolph inquired, his manner suspicious.

"I've heard about him!" Sutcliffe confirmed with a scowl, despite silently conceding there was considerable merit in the point made by the younger of the twins. Instead of mentioning that he had been puzzled in a similar fashion, on seeing how quickly his employer received the visitor, he continued, "So Fog couldn't come himself for some reason or another and he's sent somebody else!"

"If he couldn't have come himself, he'd have sent either Mark Counter, the Ysabel Kid, or at least that youngster they call 'Waco'," Aaron countered, being determined to get full value for the money paid to their companion. "And, going by everything I've heard, that runt couldn't be any one of them, any more than he's Dusty Fog!"

There was good reason for the brothers to reject the suggestion made by Sutcliffe!

Neither Rudolph nor Aaron had ever done anything to help their recently dead Uncle Cyrus, or even shown the slightest interest in his affairs while he was alive, but they had had high hopes of inheriting the fortune he had amassed. Much to their consternation, as they had believed they were his only kin, they discovered there might be somebody with a better claim to the old man's wealth. Shortly before he had died, having felt remorse over the daughter he had disowned because she married against his wishes, he had sought to rectify the situation. She was already dead, but he had hired the Pinkerton National Detective Agency to locate her only daughter. Showing their usual efficiency, the "Pink-Eyes" had done so and, as instructed, proof of her identity had been forwarded to Lawyer Horatio Greenslade in Kansas City.

Being in need of money, the brothers had been disinclined to just stand back and watch a fortune slip through their grasp. They had found a willing ally in Wilfred Stiggins, a book-keeper in their uncle's company who had need to cover his peculations. It was he who had learned that, under the terms of the will, there was a deadline set for the production of documents verifying the *bona fides* of the other claimant. Having had illicit dealings with Sutcliffe in the past, Stiggins had also suggested the means by which the presentation of the proof might be prevented. On being contacted, never averse to turning a dishonest dollar, the lawyer's clerk had stated his willingness to help provided the price for his services met with his approval.

The plan, proposed by Sutcliffe on the arrival of the brothers in Kansas City, had appeared so simple they felt it hardly justified the far from inconsiderable amount he demanded as payment. He had claimed the documents would either be sent by mail, or delivered by hand. In the former case, one of his duties was to dispatch the letter and he would see it never reached the post office. Should the latter alternative eventuate, the missive would probably be carried by the aged senior clerk, Oswald Ramsgate, and the brothers would have little difficulty in relieving him of it prior to his reaching his destination.

Unfortunately, neither contingency had occurred!

Shortly after they reached Kansas City, the brothers had received disturbing news from Stiggins. Either because he was suspicious over their sudden departure, or as a result of natural caution, their late uncle's business manager had arranged for a nephew of an old friend—General Jackson Baines "Ole Devil" Hardin, C.S.A.—who had brought a herd of OD Connected cattle from Rio Hondo County, Texas, to Newton to collect and ensure the safe arrival of the documents.

The identity of the possible collector had been the cause of grave concern!

While Rudolph and Aaron had never seen Dusty Fog, they were all too aware of his already close to legendary reputation. Being native-born Kansans, they had always pretended to discount the stories of his prowess in certain fields as no more than the bragging of his compatriots from Texas. For all that, at the bottom of their hearts, they did not doubt there was more than a little truth told about his many exploits.[2] If the stakes had been lower and their need for money less urgent—among other things, they were being pressed for payment of gambling debts by men growing increasingly insistent that it must be forthcoming —he was a person with whom they would have avoided tangling. As it was, being aware that they had no other choice if they wished to retain their health, they were determined to prevent the delivery regardless of who was carrying the documents.

Faced with the problem of identifying the carrier, although suspecting he would prove easy to pick out, the brothers had arranged for Sutcliffe to supply the solution. He claimed to have done so, but they were finding it difficult to believe his identification could be correct. To their way of thinking, it was inconceivable that the man he had indicated was Dusty Fog. In fact, they felt it highly unlikely such a person would be entrusted with so important a task.

"Damn it all!" Rudolph said, with the air of one producing indisputable proof of his assertion. "He's not even wearing a gun!"

"Kansas City isn't one of your wild and woolly towns along the railroad," Sutcliffe countered scathingly. "*Nobody* walks around *here* with a gun on his hip unless he's a police officer in uniform!" Then, because he had no desire to lose the bonus he had been promised for pointing out the

2. Details of the career, family background and special qualifications of Dusty Fog are given in: *Appendix One*. J.T.E.

man who was carrying the documents, he continued in a milder and conciliatory tone, "What if Fog, or one of those three you mentioned, couldn't make it for some reason? He might have sent that runt, figuring nobody would expect him to give such a no-account little son of a bitch the chore."

"Well—yes," Rudolph admitted, almost grudgingly, running a far from complimentary gaze over the small Texan. "Fog *might* figure it that way."

"Anyway, it has to be him who has the documents!" Sutcliffe declared. "Like I said, there hasn't been another beefhead at the office in months and old Greenslade was saying this morning it's the last day they could be collected and meet the deadline."

"All right!" the elder brother said sombrely, after a moment's silence. "We'll take your word for it!"

"There's one thing, though, Rudy," Aaron remarked, still looking disdainfully at the subject of the conversation. "If he does have them, it'll be a damned sight easier and safer taking them from him than if we were up against Dusty Fog."

"Where're you figuring on taking them?" Sutcliffe asked worriedly, being disinclined to become involved in such a criminal activity.

"On the train," Aaron replied.

"Not until we get to Newton," Rudolph contradicted.

"Why wait that long?" the dishonest clerk wanted to know.

"It'll be nightfall before we get there and he'll have to leave taking the documents to Uncle Cyrus's office until morning," the elder brother explained. "If I know cowhands, he'll make for one of the saloons and that's when we'll take him."

"It won't be so suspicious that way," Aaron supplemented. "More than one of those beefhead bastards has been found beaten over the head and robbed in an alley."

"He'll just be another, as far as anybody else will know," Rudolph went on. "Telegraph Stiggins and ask him to find out whether Fog's bunch are still in town and to meet us at the depot with some old clothes. Then we'll make that short-grown son of a bitch wish he hadn't been made interfere in our affairs."

"Here they come!" Honest Fred Defayne announced, watching the building into which the detectives had taken the Grimstons, as the last of the passengers ending their journey at Kansas City were leaving the west-bound train.

"The bulls haven't found it," Margo Defayne deduced, noticing the British couple were not handcuffed and the detectives were allowing them to walk away. "Which, knowing those two smart-assed bastards who searched 'em, they haven't got it with them."

"It looks that w—!" Defayne began. Bringing his words to a halt, he pointed like a bird dog scenting a covey of bobwhite quail. Then, having swung his gaze towards the train, he continued in an urgent tone, "Come on!"

The behaviour of the New Englander had been caused by noticing that Alfred Grimston was craning his neck and scanning the other people on the platform. Then, apparently having located the person he was seeking, he spoke to his wife and they strolled onwards. Having followed the direction in which the English criminal was looking, Defayne almost ignored the small Texan who was just boarding the day car. Suddenly remembering that Sarah Grimston had bumped into the young man as the detectives were approaching, another thought had come to him and it was this which provoked the order given to Margo.

"What's up?" the red head demanded, joining her husband as he stepped forward.

"The Duchess walked into that little feller like you do when you're high-diving a mark," Defayne explained, employing a colloquialism for picking a pocket. "And I've heard she's a pretty fair finger-smith."

"So what?" Margo inquired, watching the small Texan disappear into the car. "Even if he looked worth high-diving, she wouldn't have chanced doing it with the bulls moving in on them.'

"Not to lift anything *from* him," the New Englander conceded. "But she might've planted the Zebra on him!"

"It'd be taking a hell of a chance," the red head pointed out, glancing to where the English couple were boarding at the other end of the day car.

"No more than being caught with it on 'em would," Defayne countered. "Anyways, even if she didn't plant it on him, they'll have fixed things so it'll be sent to them and I aim to be on hand when it gets there."

On entering the day car, the New Englanders found it was not crowded and, to their satisfaction, the Texan had selected an otherwise unoccupied section of four seats. Having placed his hat and the portmanteau on the overhead baggage rack, he took the right hand window seat facing forward.

"Which pocket do you reckon he'll have it in?" Margo inquired, *sotto voce*, as she and her husband were walking along the aisle.

"I'd say the left," Defayne estimated, speaking no louder and also without appearing to move his lips.

"And me," the red head seconded. "Even if he hadn't been blocking her with his bag, he'd be less likely to reach into it for anything than on the right."

"Howdy, mister," the New Englander boomed, raising his voice and adopting a hearty, friendly tone. "Mind if me and the missus sit here?"

"No, sir," replied the small Texan, to whom the question had been addressed, glancing around and starting to rise.

"Hey now!" Defayne exclaimed, raising his right hand in a prohibitive gesture. "You don't have to leave on account of us!"

"Land's sakes, Fred!" Margo put in, smiling at the object of their attentions. "The young man's just being polite by standing up for a lady. Sit down again, mister. It's pleasant to meet a *gentleman* who knows his manners."

"*Gracias*, ma'am," the young man answered, his drawl establishing without any doubt his place of origin, doing as he was requested.

"Are you going far?" the red head asked, as she and her husband took the seats facing the Texan, wanting to estimate how much time she had to carry out an exploration of his pockets and, if it was there as they suspected, relieve him of the Zebra.

"Only to Newton by train, ma'am," the young man replied. "Then I'll be headed down the trail to home with the rest of the boys who I br—trailed north with me."

"Hey!" Margo said, seeming to exude genuine admiration and drawing a conclusion from the change made to the explanation. It concurred with the opinion she had already formed about its maker. "You must be one of those Texas *cowboys* we've heard so much about!"

"Why sure, ma'am," the Texan confirmed. He sounded proud, yet a trifle defensive as if expecting his claim to be challenged. "You could say that. I'm Edward Marsden, from Polveroso City. It's seat of Rio Hondo County 'n' I ride for the OD Connected ranch."

"*My*!" the red head uttered, sounding suitably impressed although she had never heard of the town, county, or ranch. "Isn't that *something*, Fred?"

"Excuse me for interrupting," requested a cool feminine voice with an upper class British accent, before the New

Englander could reply. "But do I understand that you are employed by a ranch in *Texas*?"

"Why sure, ma'am, the biggest and best in the whole Lone Star State," the Texan confirmed, rising and looking at the speaker. "I've been riding for the OD Connected for—well, a fair spell."

"I say, Albert," Sarah Grimston exclaimed, glancing at her husband. "How jolly *fortunate*, what?"

"It is at that, by jove, old girl!" Grimston agreed and screwed into his left eye a monocle which experience had taught him helped to establish his false claim to be a member of the British aristocracy.[3] "Best luck I've had since old Bungo Charteris and I got an all black tiger in Ranchipur."

"No tiger hunting stories, dear!" the blonde interrupted, with the air of one who had heard them all many times before. Then, diverting her attention to the couple from New England and giving no suggestion of recognizing them as fellow criminals, she went on, "Sir Albert and I are hoping to go into the ranching business in Texas ourselves, don't you know. Would we be intruding too *frightfully* if we were to sit here and discuss the prospects with this young gentleman?"

"Feel free, ma'am, or is it 'Your Highness'?" Edward Marsden authorized, without consulting the Defaynes.

"Only 'Your *Ladyship*'," Sarah corrected. "I doubt whether Her Majesty, Queen Victoria, would approve of us aspiring to one of Her titles."

"I reckon not," the Texan conceded, seeming most impressed to find himself in such exalted company even

3. While paying a visit to the United States—some details of which are recorded in: *Beguinage is Dead!*—British criminal, Amelia Penelope Diana "Benkers" Benkinsop also made use of a monocle to add a touch expected by many Americans when meeting with one they believed was a member of the English aristocracy. See, *Part Three*, *"Birds of a Feather"*, *Wanted! Belle Starr*. J.T.E.

though he did not fully comprehend what he had been told. "Anyways, I reckon I can tell you-all a few things about ranching."

Nodding graciously, the blonde took the place next to the young man and Grimston occupied the vacant seat at the other side of the aisle. Still offering no indication of knowing the American couple were other than completely law abiding citizens, she introduced herself and her husband as "Lady Sarah and Brigadier General Sir Albert Fortescue-Howard". Nor, in spite of deciding his theory was correct with regards to their connection with the small Texan, did Defayne display his appreciation of the true state affairs as he supplied the names, "Margo and Fred Gilbert" for his wife and himself.

Once the train set into motion and the conversation continued, it soon became apparent that Marsden's knowledge of the ranching business could not be considered extensive. He did not appear to have any conception of what kind of property would be best suited to the needs of the English couple, much less how much one might cost. Nor, beyond claiming his employer was "doing right well out of the spread down to home", was he able to say what financial benefits might accrue from the purchase. Questioned about how much per head cattle were currently bringing from the buyers in Newton, he was just as vague and knew only they were "fetching a whole heap more than folks in Texas used to get from 'hide and tallow men' before bringing herds north to the railroad".[4] In fact, if any of his audience had been conversant with such matters, the answer he gave when responding to an enquiry about the number of losses sustained by his outfit during the journey from their ranch

4. Information about the period and, as no other market was yet available, extremely low prices paid for cattle by hide and tallow factories in the Lone Star State is given in: *Set Texas Back on Her Feet* and *The Hide and Tallow Men.* J.T.E.

would have supplied a hint to his exact status on the trail drive.

"*They* had some get away from 'em," the small Texan admitted, in the manner of one disclaiming responsibility for a mishap on the grounds that he personally was not involved. Then his voice took on a timbre of pride as he went on, "But I *never* lost a horse!"

To anybody who was experienced in the handling of a trail herd, the boast suggested its maker had not been working directly with the cattle. Rather it implied he was employed in the menial—albeit important—capacity of wrangler, or possibly night hawk, looking after the horses in the *remuda*. To be able to claim that he had retained all the animals in his charge, rarely though it could truthfully be made due to the hazards of the long journey, was the ultimate accolade for such a person.[5]

While the others were talking, Defayne studied them with experienced eyes. Everything he saw made him more certain his theory regarding the present whereabouts of the Zebra was correct. As the Grimstons had no intention of entering the ranching business, there could be no other explanation for them using that pretence to make the Texan's acquaintance. Their interest was also unlikely to stem from the real reason for his visit to Kansas City. There were certain to have been better qualified men available to collect the papers from "Lawyer Greenslade" so obviously the documents were of no especial value. Apart from trying to decide how the Texan could be relieved of the item which the blonde had deposited on his person, the New Englander discounted him entirely as a factor in the business at hand.

Having drawn his conclusions with regards to the small Texan, Defayne found the British couple far more interest-

5. One wrangler who was able to make good the claim of never having lost a horse appears in: *Trail Boss*. J.T.E.

ing. He had frequently heard of them since their arrival in the United States, but their paths had never crossed and he would not have known who they were without having had them pointed out by a criminal associate the previous evening. As far as he could tell, the recognition was not mutual. While making it obvious that they were aware of the social difference between them, the Grimstons appeared to have accepted his explanation that Margo and he were entertainers travelling to Newton in search of employment. The appearance of the conductor saved him from the need to elaborate upon the story. Explaining to the conductor that they had all arrived at the depot in Kansas City too late to buy tickets, first the Englishman and then Defayne purchased them there and then.

Keeping just as careful a watch while the conversation was continuing in an increasingly desultory fashion, Margo saw nothing to suggest that Sarah was retrieving the Zebra from its unsuspecting carrier. Then, shortly before the sun went down, Marsden excused himself. Rising, he went to one of the small lavatory cubicles at the front end of the car. Still neither of the British criminals said or did anything to imply they were harbouring suspicions of the other couple. Instead, as Sarah and her husband continued with their pretence of being interested in the prospects of investing in the ranching business, she in particular kept a constant watch upon the door through which the small Texan had disappeared.

"Excuse me, please!" the blonde suddenly requested coming to her feet after something over three minutes had elapsed.

"I have to go myself," Margo claimed, also rising, as Sarah passed her.

On turning, the red head discovered that her guess that the small Texan had returned from the lavatory was correct!

As Sarah converged with the young man, she stumbled and, once again, they collided with one another. Studying the technique being employed, with the eyes of an accomplished pickpocket, Margo had to admit the blonde was an equally competent "finger-smith". She also discovered that her husband's estimation of where the Zebra had been placed was incorrect.

Sarah's hand disappeared into the right and not the left side pocket of the loose fitting jacket worn by Marsden!

It emerged *empty*!

Yet, in spite of having suffered what must have proved a great shock, the blonde never faltered!

Apart from a brief worried and puzzled glance over her shoulder, accompanied by a slight stiffening of her posture, Sarah continued to walk onwards as if nothing had happened!

Concluding that the small Texan must have found the Zebra whilst in the lavatory and transferred it elsewhere upon his person, Margo sought to locate it, putting to use her considerable experience as a pickpocket. First, she subjected him to a scrutiny closer than her previous one. All she ascertained was that he was more sturdily built than he gave the impression of being. Then, having failed to detect any visual clue as to the location of the Zebra with her, of necessity, brief study, she elected to conduct a closer examination by physical contact.

Being just as competent a "finger-smith" as the English-woman, the red head contrived to give the impression that the motion of the car was responsible for "accidentally" staggering against Marsden. Nevertheless, she did not attempt to put her hands into any of his pockets. Instead, regretting that time would not allow her to carry out a more thorough "bump frisk" by pressing her body against his and testing for lumps not caused by nature, she felt swiftly over the outside of his jacket's left and breast pockets. Knowing she was almost certainly being watched by Grimston, she was unable to reach around and feel at those in the Levi's.

Moving with the speed of long practice, the questing fingers failed to achieve their objective. There was what must be a bulky wallet in the right breast pocket, but she realized this was not sufficiently thick to be holding the Zebra. Nor was it anywhere else she was able to reach. Being unable to extend her examination, as to retain the close proximity with the Texan might cause the Englishman—who almost certainly possessed the knowledge to detect what she was doing—to become suspicious, she passed him and followed Sarah along the car. She wondered what Marsden had thought when he discovered what he was carrying, but felt confident that she and her husband could relieve him of it provided they could create an opportunity to separate him from the Grimstons.

Closing in upon the small Texan from the rear, Rudolph and Aaron Chufnell each caught him by a wrist and the back of his jacket collar. Having done so, they hustled him towards the entrance of the alley into which—also dressed after the fashion of a railroad construction worker—Wilfred Stiggins had already disappeared. Although much of the space between the two silent and unlit buildings was in deep shadow, there was sufficient light from the half moon for them to see that their companion was waiting in the centre for them to deliver their captive.

Fortune appeared to be favouring the brothers in their endeavours!

On their arrival at Newton, Rudolph and Aaron had found Stiggins was waiting for them at the railroad detail. Not only had he brought, in a large carpetbag the simple disguises they had requested by telegraph, he had also claimed the trail drive crew from the OD Connected ranch left town that morning. However, because their intended victim had been accompanied they had been unable to get at him earlier.

Following the group to the prestigious Columbus Grand Hotel, the conspirators had thought he was merely giving his services as a guide. Instead, accommodation had been arranged for him there. Much to their relief, he had not taken the precaution of making use of the safe behind the reception desk in which guests could have valuable items protected. Furthermore, it had seemed he was making their task easier. He had announced that, after leaving the portmanteau in his room, he meant to go to the livery barn where he had stabled his horse and make sure it would be ready for him in the morning. Although the decision had offered them an opportunity to waylay him off the premises, they had acquired quarters on the same floor in order to facilitate the retrieval of the documents if he should not be carrying them.

While changing into the clothes brought by Stiggins, the conspirators had decided upon a line of action. Slipping out of the hotel without being seen, they had waited nearby until the small Texan emerged. Knowing the town better than his companions, the book-keeper had gone ahead and the brothers followed a short distance behind their intended victim. As Stiggins had claimed would be the case, they had found the street upon which the livery barn was situated almost deserted due to the other business premises having closed for the night. Waiting until their companion selected and turned into an alley, the brothers had closed in and set about springing the trap, confident that the Texan was completely unaware of the danger. What was more, considering his size, they had no doubt that they would be able to cope with any attempt he might make to resist.

The lack of hostile response on the part of their captive as he was being forced to leave the street led the brothers to assume he was either too startled, slow witted, or frightened to resist!

Before the pair reached Stiggins, the passive behaviour came to an end!

Having performed a movement resembling that of a soldier changing step to conform with the other members of his squad, Edward Marsden braced himself against the grips upon his arms. Then, as his left foot descended, he set his weight upon it and, raising the right leg, he bent the knee until the thigh was parallel to the ground. Having done so, he drew Rudolph forward a little with a surprisingly powerful pull of the right arm and snapped the elevated limb to the rear. Driven with accuracy, the side of the boot's sole caught and raked along the front of the elder brother's shin in a most painful fashion. Letting out a yelp of pain, the recipient released his holds on the Texan and stumbled back a few steps.

Giving Aaron and Stiggins no chance to respond to the changed state of affairs, Marsden brought his right foot to the ground. Although he had removed one captor in a manner suggestive of competence, the way in which he continued acting seemed to be a bad mistake. He had swung the leg to the rear in such a fashion that his still held left arm was twisted behind his back, but this proved to be less than beneficial to the younger brother.

Before Aaron was able to take advantage of the apparent error, having clenched the liberated right fist and lifted it until level with his left shoulder, the Texan flexed his legs slightly. Swivelling to the right at the hips, his movements caused the taller man to bend at the waist. Nor was this the only effect of the pull he was exerting. It positioned the recipient to be caught in the side by the elbow of the raised arm which was propelled around. Feeling an impact on the ribs which reminded him of an occasion when he had been kicked by a horse, Aaron was compelled to let go and staggered away until colliding with the wall of the building.

Taking advantage of Marsden being preoccupied with his companions, the book-keeper bounded forward. As the younger brother was knocked clear, he enfolded the Texan's arms in his own and began to apply a bearhug. Not quite as tall as his companions, he was heavier and, despite his sedentary life, far from puny. Yet, for all his efforts to the contrary, he found the hold was being broken by a strength much greater than he had envisaged could be possessed by the diminutive intended victim. Realizing he could not achieve his purpose, an instinct for self-preservation caused him to jump backwards. Not, however, quite far enough. Coming up, Marsden's right foot thrust out to catch the centre of his chest and propel him to the opposite side of the alley where Aaron had been brought to a halt.

Snarling curses and limping slightly, Rudolph returned to the fray. Seeing the Texan was starting to turn his way, he threw a punch. It landed on the side of Marsden's jaw, driving him in a reeling sprawl across the alley. Although he was unable to keep his feet, he contrived to alight rolling in the fashion of a very competent horseman who nevertheless had been thrown by his mount. Halting by the right side wall on hands and knees, his attitude showed he was far from being incapacitated by the blow.

Even as the elder brother was shouting for his sibling and Stiggins to help and preparing to follow up his attack, there was an interruption!

"Hey!" yelled an authoritative voice.

Looking to find out who had spoken, the conspirators discovered that a man was crossing the street at the rear of the buildings. He wore range style clothing, but the moon glinted on the badge fastened to his calfskin vest and warned he was more than just a cowhand passing by chance. What was more, he was taking the precaution of arming himself by drawing his revolver as he advanced.

"Come on!" Stiggins yelled.

Needing no such advice, as they had arrived at an identical conclusion, the brothers joined the book-keeper in his flight. Despite the increased pain caused by doing so, Rudolph contrived to run as swiftly as the other two. Behind them, their intended victim began to thrust himself to his feet.

"Hold it, feller!" the peace officer commanded. As his order was obeyed he came closer and studied Marsden, then went on, "Hey, you're——!"

"I am," the small Texan replied, showing no surprise at being recognized so quickly. He no longer spoke as he had when conversing with the two couples on the train. There was a more decisive timbre to his Southern drawl and he was altogether more assertive as he continued, "Which I hope you know those three jaspers as well."

"Good evening, Mr. Marsden," Sarah Grimston greeted, rising and walking forward as the young man entered the lobby of the Columbus Grand Hotel. Overlooking the way in which he was carrying a bulky tarpaulin wrapped bed roll with no discernible effort in spite of its size, she went on, "I trust you found your horse in good health?"

"He's fit as a flea and near to as lively, Your Ladyship," the small Texan replied, having reverted to his former mode of speech. "And, now I've seen to him, I reckon I'll go out 'n' 'tend to myself as soon as I've dropped my gear in my room."

"I've always admired a man who cares for his horse before he thinks about his own welfare," the blonde claimed, walking alongside the small Texan. "Perhaps you would show Sir Albert and myself the sights tonight, unless you have other arrangements?"

"Well no, ma'am, I don't have any at all and I'd surely

admire to do it," Marsden answered, seeming to consider himself honoured by having received the offer. "Only there aren't a whole heap of 'sights' around Newton that a for-real lady like you could go and look in on."

"You'll find I'm pretty broad minded," Sarah asserted, which was true enough as far as it went. "And, anyway, a breath of fresh air won't come amiss."

While talking and accompanying Marsden upstairs, the blonde Englishwoman watched him from the corner of her eye!

At the start of the train journey, Sarah and her husband had drawn almost the same conclusions to those which, unbeknown to them, Fred Defayne was forming about the Texan. However, since her discovery that the Zebra was not in the pocket where she had dropped it to avoid being found with it in her possession when searched by the detectives in Kansas City, they had studied him more closely and had revised their assumptions. Noticing that he appeared to be practically ambidextrous had been one factor which led to their change of mind. They had considered that, if he really was what he seemed, he would have boasted of his ability as an aid to impressing them. Deciding he was far less naive than he had behaved, they had wondered whether he might be a confidence trickster of some kind and had selected them, or the rather common "Gilberts", as potential marks to be fleeced. This point of view had been enhanced when, on arriving at the hotel, it had been apparent that the reception clerk recognized him. Although the reaction had been brief and his suggestion that "Cap'n Fog was going to get me a room here" was accepted immediately, the Grimstons had not returned to believing he was the innocuous "nobody" he tried to give the impression of being.

On reaching the second floor, the thoughts Sarah was having about the possible motives of the Texan were

brought to an end. Coming from the room she was occupying with her husband, "Margo Gilbert" walked towards
them. Like the blonde, she was bare headed and she no
longer wore the feather boa.

"Hi there!" the red head said, in what appeared to be an
amiable fashion. "You wouldn't have seen that husband of
mine while you were coming back to the hotel, would you,
Mr. Marsden?"

"That's a question a feller don't rightly know how to
answer for the best, when it's asked by somebody's lady-
wife," the Texan replied, with the air of one who was trying
to give the impression of being far more worldly than
was the case. "But, seeing's as it's truthful-true, I can
come right on out and say, 'no'."

"Darn it!" Margo ejaculated. "He went out to buy some
cigars and I've just had word that the manager of the Bon
Ton Theatre wants to see one of us urgently. I don't suppose you'd take me there, Mr. Marsden, would you?"

"I'd be right honoured to do it, ma'am," the Texan declared, but kept walking in the direction he was going
when addressed, "Just let me drop my thirty-year gather-
ings off and we'll go."

"Why sure," the red head agreed, raising her voice.

"May I come along with you?" Sarah asked, also speaking louder than might have been considered necessary. "As
I told you downstairs, Mr. Marsden, I feel like taking a
breath of fresh air."

"That's all right with me," Margo assented, as the Texan
glanced in an interrogative fashion at her.

There was more than just a desire for exercise and fresh
air behind the request made by the Englishwoman. She had
been waiting in the lobby to intercept Marsden if he returned before her husband had finished searching his room.
As Albert had not joined her, she assumed the task was
taking longer than they had anticipated. However, although

he might still be in the room, she felt little concern. Even if he had not heard them coming, on hearing the click of the lock being operated, he would have time to hide either in the large wardrobe or under the bed. Provided he had not left too obvious signs of his activities, the Texan might just put down the bundle inside the door and return to the passage without becoming aware of his presence. On the other hand, should he be discovered, she was confident that he could overpower and silence such a small man and felt no doubt of her ability to do the same with the over weight red head.

Falling slightly behind the other two, so she would be able to take Margo by surprise if necessary, Sarah stood tense and ready as Marsden inserted the key in the lock and turned it. Pushing open the door, he started to enter. He had not doused the lamp suspended from the ceiling on going out and, by its illumination, was able to see the whole of his temporary quarters.

"What the hell's hap—!" the small Texan ejaculated as he crossed the threshold, coming to a halt.

Looking over Marsden's shoulders, the women each let out an equally startled and profane exclamation as they discovered the cause of his behaviour!

The room was in a state of considerable disarray!

Far more so, in fact, than even a thorough search would have left it!

The reason was obvious!

Having engaged in what was clearly a long and savage fight, Defayne was lying supine by the bed with Grimston kneeling astride his chest and throttling him!

Giving a squeal of fury, Margo pushed by Marsden and rushed forward!

Knowing her husband had entered the room to search for the Zebra, the red head had been of much the same opinion as the Englishwoman on the possibilities of the situation. What neither woman had taken into consideration was the circumstances which, due to both couples having decided upon a similar line of action, had arisen. Nor, seeing Fred in such dire straits, did Margo pause to take into account the consequences. Instead, hoisting her skirt above knee level as she advanced, she launched a kick with her shapely and muscular right leg. Caught under the chin with far from inconsiderable force by the rapidly rising high-button shoe, Grimston's head snapped back and he was pitched sideways from his unconscious opponent.

Despite having been just as shocked by the sight, although relieved to discover her husband had the upper hand, Sarah responded almost as quickly as the red head. Also having darted by the small Texan, it having been her intention to grab Margo from behind if the need had arisen, she was just too far away to prevent the kick being launched and arrived an instant after it was delivered.

Accompanying the action with a scream of rage, the blonde grabbed the red head by the shoulders and gave a surging heave. Taken unawares by the suddenness and strength of the assault, Margo felt herself being propelled backwards with a momentum which left her unable to halt the hasty involuntary retreat. In fact, she was having considerable difficulty in retaining her balance and expected to fall at any moment.

Although Margo was oblivious of the fact, she had been sent on a potential collision course towards Marsden. As he had when dealing with the shortest of his attackers in the alley a short while earlier, he displayed the surprising power possessed by his small yet remarkably sturdy frame. Without releasing the bed roll from his left hand, he raised and extended the other. Laying the right palm against the back of the rapidly approaching woman, in spite of her being somewhat larger and heavier than himself, he brought her to a stop without any noticeable difficulty.

Finding herself being halted in a much less painful way than she had anticipated, Margo did not waste any time in trying to ascertain how this had been brought about. Instead, she plunged forward and was met halfway across the room by Sarah. Two pairs of hands sank eagerly into hair and started pulling. They spun around, locked together by the grips they had taken. Then the extra weight of the red head and their mutually incautious movements caused them to stagger until they tripped over her recumbent and immobile husband. Landing upon the equally unresisting Grimston broke the force of their fall, but did nothing to stop them fighting.

Watching the women rolling around the floor with legs flailing wildly and hands jerking at hair, Marsden gave a shake of his head indicative of puzzlement. He had formed certain conclusions about the reason why one or both couples had sought to make his acquaintance on the train, so had taken steps to try them out. Considering what he had found on returning to his room, he wondered if each pair had the same motive unbeknown to the other. However, instead of trying to intervene and solve the mystery, he stepped into the passage and closed the door behind him.

Having laid the bed roll on the floor and turned the key he had left in the lock, the Texan started to walk towards the stairs. Before he reached them, he saw three men coming from a room at the other side of the passage. Two were clearly closely related, the one on the left limping a little, and the third was shorter and older. All were bare headed and wore respectable suits, shirts, ties and footwear such as might be expected of residents in such a good quality hotel.

For some reason, each of the trio was keeping his right hand concealed behind his back!

Having made good their escape, without being pursued by the peace officer or their intended victim, the conspirators had managed to return unchallenged to their room at the Columbus Grand Hotel and hold a council of war.

Finding the brothers were equally disinclined to give up the attempt to prevent the delivery of the documents, Wilfred Stiggins had proposed a plan which neither Rudolph nor Aaron Chufnell had been able to better. He claimed it was unlikely the small Texan had had time to take a close look at their faces and might believe they were no more than ordinary robbers, so they would have a better chance of catching him by surprise at the hotel. Certainly he would be less alert there than if found again on the streets. All they had to do was keep watch on the passage and select the most suitable moment to go out and tackle him.

Changing into clothing more suitable for their surroundings, the trio had put the plan into effect. When their intended victim had made his appearance, having the women with him had prevented them from taking any action. However, the book-keeper had insisted the observation was continued. Although puzzled by his behaviour on emerging alone from his room, they had decided to make the most of the opportunity. Remembering how effectively he had defended himself in the alley, they had felt it was most inadvisable to rely upon bare hands to subdue him. To avoid the need to do so, each was carrying one of the revolvers which Stiggins had had the forethought to supply along with their disguises. They were confident that, particularly as the small Texan did not appear to be armed in any way, he would have no choice other than to surrender when confronted by their weapons.

"Now!" the book-keeper snapped, when satisfied he and his companions were close enough. He started to bring the revolver from behind his back.

Being basically simple, the plan was good!

However, to achieve success, the intended victim was

required to be taken unawares and too startled, or frightened, to resist!

Edward Marsden quickly proved he lacked all the necessary qualities!

While Stiggins had been correct when assuming the small Texan had not been able to see the faces of the attackers in the alley with any clarity, he had assessed their general appearances. He was aware that, despite being dressed differently, the three men who were approaching possessed the general physical requirements to be his former assailants. Two of them also fitted another point. On learning what was wanted of him on his mission, he had been informed that the beneficiaries with most to lose if delivery of the documents was successful were twin brothers. Added to that, he was aware of how much pain was inflicted by the kind of stamping kick he had delivered to free himself from the first of his assailants. Noticing the slight limp affecting the gait of the man on the left gave further support to his suppositions.

Lastly and most significant to Marsden's way of thinking, was the way in which each man had his right hand concealed from view!

Having drawn his conclusions quickly, the Texan was alert to the possibility of there being another attempt to relieve him of the documents!

However, although Marsden had given no sign of it during the previous encounter, he was far from being as defenseless against an armed attack than was envisaged by the would-be robbers!

The moment Stiggins gave the order, the Texan began to discredit the misconception with great rapidity!

Rising and working with the smooth co-ordination which told of considerable practice, Marsden's left hand grasped the near side lapel of the baggy jacket and drew it open so the right could disappear beneath it. Making a twisting motion, the latter emerged almost immediately grasping a short barreled Webley Royal Irish Constabulary revolver. The moment that the British-made weapon was clear, the left hand released the jacket and joined its mate on the butt. Brought to shoulder height and extended at arms' length, the Webley was sighted and the double-action trigger depressed to send the .455 calibre bullet on its way in less than a second of the draw being commenced.

Selected as the most dangerous of the trio, as it was he who had instigated the attack, the book-keeper was hit between the eyes a split second before his weapon could be turned into alignment on the small Texan. Thrown backwards and killed instantly, he was prevented from getting off a shot.

Nor did either of the brothers fare any better!

Turning while the double handed hold was counteracting the far from inconsiderable recoil kick, seemingly of its own volition, the mechanism of the Webley functioned again and sent lead into the centre of Rudolph's chest. Even as the elder brother was going down, Marsden was once more swinging his revolver. His actions were those of an exceptionally competent gun fighter.

Although Aaron had been granted an opportunity to bring around and point his weapon, two things combined to unnerve him!

In addition to the devastatingly effective gun play being witnessed by the younger brother, in some strange way, the Texan ceased to strike him as being small and insignificant. Rather Marsden appeared to have grown until looming far larger than him. Startled by this apparent metamorphosis, which he realized later must have been produced by the strength of Marsden's personality, he fired. His haste caused him to miss. There was no chance to try and correct his aim. For the third time, the British revolver—designed for ease of concealment—moved and thundered. Struck in the right shoulder, Aaron twirled on his heels. The hand-gun fell from his grasp and, shrieking in pain, he collapsed against the wall.

"Seems like I've been doing all you good folks an injustice," declared the young man who had introduced himself as "Edward Marsden" on the train, as he entered the cell block of the jailhouse accompanied by the town marshal of Newton, "I thought one pair or the other of you-all was set on stopping me delivering some documents I'd collected from Counsellor Greenslade in Kansas City. Only we've just been told different by one of the jaspers who were trying to do it."

The words were directed at Sarah Grimston and Margo Defayne as they sat in adjoining cells. Until they saw who had entered, they had been glowering through the bars at each other. Both were dishevelled, scratched and bruised. Their badly tangled hair and torn clothing still clung wetly to them. This had come about as a result of the soaking from two buckets of cold water poured over them by the Texan and the house detective at the Columbus Grand Hotel in order to end what had been a long, very rough and not yet concluded fight. Brought to the scene by the shooting in the passage, the marshal had arranged for the women and their husbands to be taken to the jailhouse. Although something over half an hour had elapsed, such was the extent of their injuries, the men were still receiving medical attention from a doctor.

"Don't give me that shit!" the blonde screamed, rising to grab and shake at the bars of her cell's door in anger. All trace of upper class elegance had left her, even her accent having coarsened. "You know why we were after you, damn it. You've got the 'mother-something' Zebra!"

"'*Zebra*', Your Ladyship?" Marsden repeated, looking puzzled. He no longer conveyed an impression of naive insecurity. As had been the case with Aaron Chufnell, he appeared to have become larger, somewhat older and far more mature, exuding an air of command which had not previously been in evidence. "I've heard tell of them, I'll admit. But I've never seen one, much less—!"

"Don't try to weasel out of it, you bastard!" Sarah interrupted. Too furious to draw any conclusions from the change which had come over the Texan, she failed to appreciate how it gave confirmation to her suspicion that he might not be what he seemed on the surface. "I dropped the bloody thing in your jacket pocket at the railway station in Kansas City and you found it while you were in the lavatory!"

"I didn't, ma'am," Marsden contradicted calmly, turning the pockets inside out to show they were empty. "And there's nothing in them."

"Not now there ain't!" Margo conceded, having come to the door of her cell. Sharing the determination of the blonde to prevent the young man from making a profit out of their mutual misfortune, she went on heatedly, "You found it and've got it stashed away somewheres else!"

"No, ma'am, I *haven't* and—!" Marsden commenced, then he looked down. "Hold hard, though!"

"What's up, Cap'n?" the marshal inquired, looking at the Texan in a more respectable fashion than might seem warranted by external appearances.

"I knew I wouldn't be able to wear my gunbelt in Kansas City and, the reason I was going there, I didn't take over kind to the notion of travelling naked. So I borrowed this jacket from Cousin Red because it's baggy enough to hide my shoulder holster and Webley hide-out gun."

While speaking, the young man was examining the lining of the right side pocket. Showing there was a hole in it, he removed and began to feel around the bottom of the jacket. Mutual exclamations of annoyance burst from

Sarah and Margo as they realized what must have happened. Giving a grunt of satisfaction, Marsden enlarged the hole and reached through the gap.

"Whee dogie!" the peace officer ejaculated, staring at the Texan's hand as it emerged. "Will you just take a look at those!"

The objects in question were a double string of matched and alternating black and white pearls!

"So this's what you call the 'Zebra', huh?" Marsden said quietly.

"You know damn well it is!" Sarah confirmed, staring covetously at the necklace she and her husband had stolen the previous evening from the wife of a railroad tycoon, unknowingly circumventing similar intentions on the part of the Defaynes. Then, having turned a gaze filled with hatred at the small Texan, she directed her next words at the marshal. "Don't tell me you *believe* he didn't know the bloody thing was there?"

"Do you know who this is, ma'am?" the peace officer inquired.

"He told us his name's Edward Marsden!" the blonde replied.

"And so it is, ma'am," the young man declared. "I was baptized 'Dustine Edward Marsden'. Only, not wanting to scare off any of you good folks until I was sure whether you hadn't got the notion of taking the documents I was toting away from me, I left off the 'Dustine' and didn't mention my surname, which's 'Fog'."

"So your real name's Dustine Edward Marsden Fog," Sarah answered, wondering why she thought there was something significant about the information she had just acquired. Again she swung her attention to the marshal, "But that doesn't mean he didn't know the Zebra was there and intended to keep it."

"Yeah," Margo supported. "He knew it was there all right!"

"He says he *didn't*," the peace officer stated, as if considering the declaration closed the matter. "And the word of Cap'n Dusty Fog is good enough for me."

PART TWO

The Invisible Winchester

"Well, we're almost there at *last*," remarked Marvin Eldridge "Doc" Leroy, nodding towards the open main gates of Fort Sorrell. Then, directing what appeared to be a glare of righteous indignation at his companion, he went on, "Now don't you *dare* go laying the blame on *me*, you varmint. It was *you*, not *me*, said we should stop over for a spell and sit in on that friendly 'n' honest lil poker game with Sandy, 'stead of coming straight here like you was told."

"Shucks, I'm not worrying at all over being a couple of days late," claimed the youngster whose only known name was "Waco".[1] Fact being, as soon's we get there, I'm going right up to Dusty all straight-forward and honourable—and lie my god-damned head off over how come."

"It won't do any use," Doc warned. "He'll know you're lying for sure."

"How?"

"He'll see your lips moving!"

"Now was I to think some about *that*," Waco drawled,

1. Details of the family background, career and special qualifications of Waco and Marvin Eldridge "Doc" Leroy are given in: *Appendix Four*. J.T.E.

his accent—like that of his companion—proving birth and upbringing had been in Texas. "In two-three weeks at *most*, I'd maybe come up with the notion's how you're saying I tend to stretch the truth a lil mite once in a while."

"You'd be *wrong*," Doc contradicted. "I was saying that you do it all the time."

Anybody who was conversant with the ways of Westerners in general and Texas' cowhands in particular and had overheard the comments passing between the pair would have deduced they were good friends. Otherwise, the implication by one that the other was a liar would almost certainly have ended in gun play. However, there was no doubt left by their appearance and clothing—or the low horned, double girthed range saddles, each with a lariat strapped to the horn, bulky tarpaulin warbag and leather chaps fastened to the cantle and Winchester Model of 1873 rifle in the boot attached to the right side, butt forward to allow easy removal on dismounting—that they belonged to that hard-working, harder-playing section of the population.

Taller and younger of the riders, Waco was in his late 'teens. Wide shouldered, lean of waist and with a powerful physique, he was blond haired, clean shaven and handsome. From the low crowned, wide brimmed black hat on his head, through a red bandana, dark blue shirt, brown and white calfskin vest and Levi's pants, to the boots on his feet, with Kelly spurs on their heels, his attire signified he was a son of the Lone Star State. Around his middle, a well designed brown *buscadero* gunbelt carried a brace of staghorn handled Colt Artillery Model Peacemaker revolvers in holsters intended—provided the wearer possessed the requisite skill to utilize the quality, which he did—to allow them to be brought out with great speed. Although it would have been inadvisable for anybody other than an expert horseman to take such a liberty, he sat a big paint stallion bearing the CA brand of Clay Allison's ranch in a seemingly relaxed fashion.

At around six foot, lacking some two inches of his companion's height, and about five years older, Doc was more slender in build although far from being skinny or puny. His good looking face suggested a much more serious mien than was the case. However, while pallid, this was because his skin resisted tanning rather than through leading a sedentary and indoor existence. His hair was black, recently trimmed as was the neat moustache which graced his top lip. With one exception, he was dressed in the same general fashion as the blond. Instead of having a vest, he had on a loose fitting brown jacket. Its right side was stitched back to offer unimpeded access to the ivory butt of the solitary Colt Civilian Model Peacemaker in the holster of a black gunbelt, also intended to permit the very rapid withdrawal of the weapon. The easy way in which he sat his large black horse was indicative of a similar competence in matters equestrian. There was a small black bag, of the kind in which doctors carry the tools of their profession, suspended from his saddle-horn on the opposite side to the coiled lariat.

Regardless of the comments they had been exchanging, neither Texan believed there was any reason for concern over the delay in their arrival!

When Captain Dustine Edward Marsden "Dusty" Fog heard what had led to the decision to stay at the ranch owned by a friend of long standing, Sandy McGraw,[2] he would raise no objections. They had learned of losses being incurred by the rancher and had joined in a poker game where their combined knowledge of crooked gam-

2. The connection between Captain Dustine Edward Marsden "Dusty" Fog and Sandy McGraw is explained in various volumes of the *Civil War* series and *McGraw's Inheritance*. J.T.E.

bling had established that the play was less than friendly
and far from honest. In fact, the message received by Waco
as he was preparing to leave at the successful conclusion of
his duties as temporary deputy sheriff of Clinton County
had merely been to tell him where he could join the other
members of the OD Connected ranch's floating outfit.[3]

By a fortunate coincidence, Doc had also brought to an
end the private business upon which he had been engaged.
This had led to a reunion with the blond youngster and was
now allowing them to travel together. However, after he
had called at Fort Sorrel to pay his respects to Dusty, Mark
Counter and the Ysabel Kid, he planned to go in search of
the outfit for whom he worked. Instead of delivering cattle
to the shipping pens of the rail-road in Kansas, (under their
contract to small ranchers lacking sufficient stock to send a
trail herd individually,[4]) the Wedge were handling something so unusual he was eager to play a part in it.[5]

Even without the inducement of an opportunity to renew
his acquaintance with three more good friends, Doc had been
far from averse for having a reason to visit Fort Sorrel. Over
the past few weeks, one topic had started to receive prominence in newspapers and general conversation everywhere
his travels had taken him. Knowing how the Wedge might be
affected should the outcome develop as was all too frequently being suggested, he felt sure his employer, Martin
Jethro "Stone" Hart, would be only too pleased to be told all
he could find out regarding the situation.

3. Why Waco was serving as a temporary deputy sheriff in Clinton
County, Texas, is told in: *Part Five, "The Hired Butcher", The Hard
Riders* and *Part Four, "A Tolerable Straight Shooting Gun", The Floating
Outfit.* We would like to point out that the various episodes in this book
do not run in chronological sequence. J.T.E.
4. Martin Jethro "Stone" Hart and his Wedge trail crew make "guest"
appearances in: *Quiet Town, Trigger Fast* and *Gun Wizard.* J.T.E.
5. The unusual nature of the assignment being handled by the Wedge trail
crew is described in: *Buffalo Are Coming!* J.T.E.

Reaching the gate of the Fort, a need to explain the reason for their visit to the sentry brought an end to the light-hearted conversation before anything more could be said upon the subject which the two young Texans were discussing.

"Why howdy there, Paddy!" Waco greeted, as he and his companion were allowed to pass through the main entrance. While speaking, he raised his right hand in a gesture of friendly salutation to the ruddy featured, tall and burly Cavalry non-commissioned officer who left the group on the porch of the guardhouse. "You've come up in the world a mite since the last time our trails crossed."

"Sure now and wasn't it all done by good and sober living?" replied Sergeant Major Seamus Patrick "Paddy" Magoon, his promotion having been achieved since the last occasion which had brought himself and the blond youngster into contact.[6] Glancing behind the newcomers, he frowned and continued in his rich Irish brogue, "And where might Cap'n Dusty, Mark and the Kid be?"

"You mean they aren't *here*?" Waco asked.

"That they aren't," Magoon confirmed. "And it's impatient Himself's getting—!"

"Blast it, Doc!" the blond youngster ejaculated, without even wondering to which "Himself" the non-com was referring, but glaring with what appeared to be wrath at the slender, pallid featured Texan. "Didn't I say's how there wasn't no need for us to rush off from Sandy's place, 'cause they wouldn't't've made it here yet?"

"You *didn't*," the Wedge hand replied. "Which I don't

6. Some information regarding the career of Sergeant Major Seamus Patrick "Paddy" Magoon, United States' Cavalry, can be found in: *The Rushers* and *Apache Rampage*. However, when describing a meeting he had with Miss Martha "Calamity Jane" Canary—due to an error in the source of reference from which we were producing the manuscript—we inadvertently referred to him as "Paddy Muldoon"; .see: *Trouble Trail*. J.T.E.

reckon for even a moment's going to stop you trying to lay the blame on poor innocent lil ole me!"

"It won't" Waco asserted, his manner unabashed. "That's what poor innocent lil ole friends're for, isn't it?"

"Why don't you rest them comfortable armchairs's you Texans call saddles?" Sergeant Major Magoon suggested, before Doc Leroy could reply to the blond youngster's question. "And I'll take you to my Company's lines, so's you can put up your hosses."

"*Gracias*, Paddy," Waco assented, dismounting and glancing around. "Nice place you've got here."

"It's not much," the non-com answered, sounding in spite of his bulk and rock hard demeanour like a young bride employing false depreciation as she displayed her new premises to friends. "But we call it home sweet home."

Designed with the need of a permanent base for members of the United States' Cavalry in mind, Fort Sorrel was surrounded by an adobe wall some twenty feet high. This was in the form of a square, having a parapet wide enough to allow weapons to be used through its embrasures and with access attainable at gates on each side. Barracks and stables lined two edges of the massive central parade ground, the third being given over to quarters for married personnel of all ranks. To the left, flanking the main entrance, were buildings containing various types of military equipment and supplies and the premises of the post sutler. At the right, beyond the guardhouse, were the regimental offices and accommodation for single officers or those unaccompanied by their wives. In a corner beyond the sutler's combined saloon and general store was a small, square adobe cabin which was clearly of recent construction.

"What's doing hereabouts, Paddy?" Waco inquired as he and Doc, who had also swung to the ground, set off leading their horses and accompanied by the burly noncom.

Indicating the crowded hitching rail outside the sutler's building, with most of the tethered animals bearing civilian instead of military types of saddle, he went on, "Seems like you've got more than your share of visitors calling."

"That we have," Magoon admitted. "Word got out quicker than we counted on, or wanted, so there's a powerful lot of fellers come here interested in hearing what ole Ten Bears's got to say."

"*Ten Bears!*" the blond youngster repeated, coming as close as he ever did to inadvertantly showing surprise. "Would that be the same Ten Bears as's *paria:vo* of the *Kweharehnuh* Comanch'?"

"The very self same one!" the sergeant major confirmed, being aware that "*paria:vo*" meant senior "old man", or "peace" chief—as opposed to a fighting leader —of the *Kweharehnuh*, Antelope, band of the Comanche nation. "And wasn't it his-self's come in not a week gone saying's he wanted to make peace talk."

"Whee-dogie!" Waco ejaculated. "Don't that just get you kissed off the cushion?"

"It's no wonder you've got a whole slew of callers," Doc asserted. "Hey though, Ten Bears coming in right now's like' to get you thinking he's been reading the same newspapers that I have."

"Why'd that be, *amigo*?" the blond asked.

"When I was coming through, some feller was writing in the *Ulvalde Clarion* saying's how it was time the State Legislature and Congress got around to having the *Kweharehnuh* run out of the Palo Duro country," the slender Texan explained. "And how Ten Bears, as their 'big chief', should be strung up for having personally done meanness to 'n' killed off his poor white-haired old grandmomma along the Trinity back in 'Sixty-One."

"There's *some* who'd say he'd got call to be riled,"

Waco commented, in a way which drew the eyes of his companions to him.

"Most anybody would be, given such circumstances," Doc conceded. "Which, seems like, somebody else had been. Another feller was saying the exact same thing in the *San Angelo Standard* when I got there."

"His name wouldn't've been 'Brandon', would it?" the blond said, apparently in an off-hand fashion.

"Neither him, nor the jasper over to Ulvalde," the slender Texan replied and, although sure he could guess the answer, queried, "Why?"

"'Cause a jasper giving the name 'Ezekiel Brandon' wrote practically the same letter in the *Clinton Echo* just before I pulled out," Waco claimed. "*Could* be's they was all three of them kin."

"It *could* be at that," Magoon put in, showing what was equally apparent cynicism to anybody who knew him, or were as skilful at playing poker as the two young Texans. "Trouble being, to the best of my recollection, the Trinity River's just a *teensy* few hundred miles further east than the *Kweharehnuh* ever raided. Why, there's even some's might reckon thereabouts wasn't even Comanch' stomping grounds at all, but Kiowa."

"Heavens to Betsy!" Waco gasped, apparently struck by a thought he could hardly credit being true. "Do you mean's how all those three *hombres* might be blaming the wrong feller *deliberate*', for shame?"

"Lands sakes, a-mercy!" Doc went on, so seriously he too might not have believed such a thing was possible. "Whatever'd make even *you* think a thing like *that*, *amigo*?"

"Well now," the blond drawled. "I'm not gainsaying there is an Ezekiel Brandon in Clinton County, only he was away on vacation when the letter was shoved under the *Echo's* front door. When I read it and asked, the editor allowed he'd never thought of good ole Ezekiel being out of town and only put it in because there was some space left over and the Brandon Feed Barn was a regular advertiser."

"Now was I as suspicious-natured as *some* I could name, but *won't*," the slender cowhand declared, the direction in which he gazed pointedly offering a clue as to the identify of at least one. "I *could* get around to thinking's that was just a lil mite *suspicious*."

"Such a mean and untrusting thing wouldn't *never* have occurred to *me*!" Waco claimed, exuding a conscious virtue which appeared genuine even though neither of his companions believed this to be the case. "Anyways, even *if* it was ole Ten Bears who did meanness to and killed off all them different fellers' poor white-haired grand-mommas along the Trinity back to Sixty-One, stringing him up now he's come in ready to make peace talk don't strike a half-smart Texas boy like me's showing right good sense. Doing it'll mean the only way to fetch the rest of the *Kweharehnuh* out of the Palo Duro, like's being asked, will be at the point of a gun. Which, going by all I've heard and seen of Comanch', they won't take kind' to such even being *tried*."

"I'll say 'amen' to that!" the burly sergeant major declared fervently. "Only them's never saw war whoops riled up and on the rampage would want anything doing's might start it up, even if it'd stop with the *Kweharehnuh*, or just them and the other Comanch' bands. Which *we* all know it *won't*!"

"No more than water'll stop running down a slope, nor the rest going when a few steers in a trail herd starts to stampede," the blond agreed. "Now me, I could go until I die, get my wings and head for heaven, without seeing more fuss with Indians of any kind, much less having it from *every* kind as'd happen should the *Kweharehnuh* take the war path."

"Happen *you* get wings and head for heaven when you die," Doc scoffed, despite having identical sentiments on the subject of avoiding Indian hostilities. "You'll surely spoil it for all those good Christian folks's have worked hard and lived right 'n' proper to get there."

"It'd make me wish's how I'd been a miserable sinner, a-drinking and carousing all his life," Magoon supported, "'stead of living sober 'n' upright, doing good deeds."

Regardless of the levity which none could resist injecting into the conversation, the two young Texans and the older, more experienced sergeant major could visualize the implications behind what they were discussing!

All three were aware that, even if there was not being waged a deliberate campaign to arouse public support and bring about the forcible expulsion of the *Kweharehnuh*, hardly anybody throughout the Lone Star State would be left unmoved by the possibilities which the unexpected arrival of Chief Ten Bears at Fort Sorrel suggested.

In general, the trio considered the reaction would prove favourable!

Unlike the other bands of the Nemenuh, feeling confident in the security offered by their stronghold in the wild Palo Duro country, the *Kweharehnuh* had declined when offered the opportunity to sign a peace treaty and be transferred to a reservation.[7] Instead, while considerably restricted in the amount of space available for their wanderings, they had returned to their hunting grounds and retained much of their traditional free-ranging way of life. Apart from having reached an agreement which permitted a bunch of badly wanted fugitives from justice to build a town deep in their territory, they had generally sought to avoid any contact with people who did not belong to their

7. Told in: *Sidewinder*. J.T.E.

race. Even after the removal of the community of outlaws, in which Waco had played a part,[8] they had continued with their policy of keeping to themselves and making no trouble beyond the bounds of their terrain.

Nevertheless, to anybody who knew Indians, there had always been two major possibilities of conflict arising!

Trespass by white people upon the domain of the *Kweharehnuh*, whether by accident or design, could cause the required incident!

Just as certainly, so could braves deciding life was growing too tame and electing to resume riding the war trail which had once brought acclaim to the participants as a result of coups being counted and loot gathered to be shared with those less fortunate!

With such considerations in mind, many older residents of Texas and other long serving members of the United States' Army within the boundaries of the State, in addition to the trio, would welcome the suggestion of peaceful negotiations from Chief Ten Bears. They believed such talks were infinitely preferable to trying to coerce the *Kweharehnuh* into quitting the Palo Duro country. Their memories were all too vivid regarding the days of Indian hostilities, when the Comanche in particular laid waste to the land and took many lives. Should their domain be subjected to armed invasion, the Antelope braves would not restrict themselves to merely fighting and were certain to strike at civilians as well as the military sent against them.

What was more, the same group of knowledgeable public opinion had long been aware of an ever present danger from another source posed by the *Kweharehnuh* remaining at liberty. With them to serve as a reminder, there would always be the temptation for warriors languishing in boredom on reservations to consider that a return to the old way

8. Told in: *Hell in the Palo Duro* and *Go Back to Hell*. J.T.E.

of life was desirable and take to the war path to bring this about. However, if the Antelope band should come in and join them, especially as a result of suggestions by the *paria:vo* rather than the white men, the risk would be reduced.

The Texans and the soldier also appreciated that, while probably approving of the reasons which had brought Ten Bears to Fort Sorrel, another section of the community were likely to be considering the situation in a far less altruistic fashion even if they were not actually involved in the campaign they had been discussing. Raising cattle in large numbers, particularly free-ranging and, at best, only semi-domesticated longhorns, required a great deal of grazing land. In spite of the enormous acreage already offered by Texas, this was growing increasingly difficult to obtain. However, with the Palo Duro country no longer closed by the *Kweharehnuh* band—who had summarily evicted the previous, less warlike dwellers therein—a further area of considerable size would become available for ranching. Therefore, speculators—many of whom were not native born Texans, the very lucrative cattle raising business having attracted investment from outside the State—could be counted upon to keep an eye upon the developments.

"Anyways, *amigo*," Doc remarked, before Waco could protest against the insinuations that he was an unsuitable candidate for heaven, "Now we know why Dusty was asked to fetch you varmints from the OD Connected out here."

"Why'd that be?" the blond youngster asked.

"'Cause Ten Bears asked for you to be on hand," the slender cowhand explained. "Could be, him not knowing any better, he figured you-all would be good folks to have siding him."

"And he'd be rightful right about *that*," Waco asserted, with well done false modesty. "Only Dusty, Mark 'n' Lon were already headed here afore he came in."

"Hell, yes!" Doc conceded, impressed as always by the way in which—the levity notwithstanding—his young companion would draw correct conclusions from what he saw or heard. "Why were they sent for, Paddy?"

"I wouldn't be knowing the all of it me-self," Magoon admitted. "But I'd be saying it's something *big*, seeing's how General Philo Handiman his own self's come hot-footed all the way from Washington, D.C., to take a hand in it."

"General Handiman!" Waco ejaculated. "But he's the big augur of—!"

"Aye, that he is," the sergeant major affirmed, despite the comment having come to a halt unconcluded. He was pleased by the way in which the blond had refrained from mentioning that General Philo Handiman was the current head of the United States' Secret Service. However, he was also aware the reticence was not caused by a lack of trust in the discretion of the slender cowhand, but had been brought about through a realization that such information could not be divulged without authorization even to a good friend. "Anyways, most likely Himself'll be telling you all about it. He left word at the guardhouse for you fellers to be fetched to him as soon's you got here. So, after you've put your hosses up, that's what I'll be doing."

"Hey now!" Waco said, gesturing ahead with his empty left hand, as he and Doc Leroy were being taken to meet General Handiman. "Isn't that ole Ten Bears his-self coming?"

Having arrived at the stable block allotted to the Company for which Paddy Magoon was sergeant major, while discussing the situation which had brought them to Fort Sorrel, the Texans had placed their horses in empty stalls. With the immediate needs of the animals satisfied, something no cowhand worth his salt would neglect except in the direst emergency, they had accepted the suggestion from the burly non-com that they leave behind their belongings until learning whether they were to be accommodated with the enlisted men or in "officers country."

Although their saddles had been placed in the care of an elderly corporal with the bed rolls still attached to the cantles, the young blond and his slender *amigo* were holding the rifles from the boots as they emerged from the building. Despite the arrangements he had made for the safekeeping of their other property, Magoon did not consider this was in any way an unspoken reflection upon the honesty of the men under his command. Being equally well informed on such matters, he knew that nobody having had the Texans' lifelong acquaintance with firearms would leave unattended one which was loaded. This was particularly the case with a Winchester Model of 1873 which, provided there was a round in the chamber and the tubular magazine beneath the barrel was filled to capacity, could be discharged seventeen times in very rapid succession.

The sergeant major was escorting the visitors towards the regimental headquarters, to ascertain the whereabouts of General Handiman. Even before Waco had asked the question, he too had noticed the tall, bulky, white haired and clearly elderly Indian—part of whose attire was made from the hide of pronghorn antelope peculiar to the *Kweharehnuh* Comanche instead of the more usual buckskin approaching across the parade ground. Although he was not clad in his full regalia, or armed in any way, he had a dignity of carriage befitting the *paria:vo* of a proud band of warriors who still retained their liberty.

"Aye, 'tis Ten Bears all right," Magoon confirmed, but with a frown coming to his rugged face. "Only he's not supposed to be wandering about on his lonesome!"

Having suspected such might be the case, the confirmation of his supposition caused the young blond to take his

attention from Ten Bears. Two factors which had already
served him well when acting as a peace officer were his
inborn powers of observation, and his retentive memory.
Recollecting something which had registered upon his sub-
conscious while going to the stables, he swung his gaze
towards the post sutler's building to verify it. Sure enough,
unlike the other animals awaiting their owners, the horse
standing nearest to the main entrance had its reins draped
over instead of being tied to the hitching rail. While this
indicated a reasonably high standard of training, the fact
that it allowed a hurried departure if necessary was also
known to him.

Satisfied his memory had not been at fault, Waco looked
next at the building. He discovered several men were
standing just inside the main entrance. Saying something
which the youngster could not hear to the others, one of the
group suddenly lurched through the batwing doors. Tall
and lean, he was shaggy haired, unshaven, clad in none too
clean range clothing and wearing a low hanging holster
carrying a Colt Civilian Model Peacemaker. The way in
which he was moving suggested he could have been drinking "not wisely, but too well." Teetering from the porch, he
was staring fixedly at the *Kweharehnuh* "peace" chief.

"That's the stinking son-of-a-bitch's killed my poor ole
grandmomma!" the man bellowed in what appeared to be a
whiskey-slurred voice and with an accent more Northern
than Texan. Reaching for the revolver, he went on, "And
I'm going to pay him back for doing it right now!"

Already alert for trouble, the possibility having been
suggested by his flair for deductive reasoning, Waco did
not doubt the threat would be carried out. Therefore, he
knew something must be done and it must be actions, not
merely words. However, his instinct for such things
warned him that the distance between himself and the
would-be vengeance seeker was too great to permit accu-

rate intervention with a handgun. Fortunately, he was not compelled to rely upon his holstered revolvers.

Even as the man commenced the draw, the youngster was whipping the Winchester upwards. With his left hand closing upon the wooden foregrip, he felt grateful that he had not rendered the weapon "safe" by unloading it before leaving the stable. There had been a time when he would not have thought twice before sending the bullet into the man's head. Since those days, he had learned when it was advisable to shoot in a less fatal fashion if possible. Realizing this was such an occasion, he was deciding how to do so as his right hand around the wrist of the butt was guiding the metal plate to nestle against his shoulder. Aligning the sights as carefully as the urgency of the situation would allow, on squeezing the trigger, his instincts as a marksman warned he would not hit his selected target.

Nevertheless, the shot achieved the desired effect!

Thrust along the rifling grooves of the twenty-six inch octagonal barrel, driven by the volume of gas created from detonating forty grains of prime Du Pont black powder, the flat-nosed .44 calibre bullet flew to attain a much more fortunate result than any young Texan could hope for in his lifetime. Its passage was slightly higher and farther out than intended, for which the lean man might have counted himself lucky. Striking the frame of the revolver, the impact tore the weapon from his grasp with a force which broke his triggerfinger; but he could easily have been far worse off. The lead might have ripped through the thigh at which it was directed, or could have hit and caused the bullets in the cylinder to explode. As it was, despite giving a pain filled howl and dropping to his knees, clutching the injured right hand with his left, he was comparatively unharmed.

Disturbed by the commotion, the horses at the hitching rail began to move restlessly. However, although it backed away until its reins fell from the rail, the animal which was not fastened made no attempt to bolt.

"Hold it right there, all of you!" Magoon thundered, starting to run forward as the rest of the group by the front entrance began to leave the sutler's building.

Throwing the lever of his Winchester through its re-loading cycle, Waco kept his attention upon the man at whom he had shot while accompanying the sergeant major and Doc. Either in response to Magoon's command, or because they saw the slender Texan holding his rifle in a position of readiness, the emerging group came to a halt instead of leaving the porch. They wore civilian clothing of various styles and levels of value. Although a couple were carrying revolvers in plain view, neither made any attempt to try and arm himself.

"Leave it lie!" Waco snapped, swinging the barrel of his Winchester towards the kneeling man.

"God damn it!" the would-be killer of the *paria:vo* spat out, but halted the movement of his left hand towards the Peacemaker which had commenced when he realized he was not seriously injured. Raising his hate-filled gaze beyond the muzzle of the rifle which was being directed with disconcerting steadiness at the centre of his chest, he glared at the blond youngster and went on as if unable to believe such a thing possible, "You *shot* me!"

"Only your gun," Waco corrected, noticing the drunken slur had left the speaker's voice. "And, seeing's how you was fixing to throw down on Chief Ten Bears, it seemed like a right smart thing to do."

"There was a time when killing a Comanche was con-sidered the 'right smart thing to do'," called the best dressed of the men on the porch.

"Why sure," the blond admitted, glancing at the speaker. Of just over middle height, plump rather than burly, in his early forties, he had a sun reddened and somehow blandly honest cast of features. His attire was in the latest city fashion and he did not wear any discernible weapons. "Only that was when they was riding the war trail. Seeing's how the chief there's come in to talk peace of his own free will and isn't toting any weapons, I've stopped that jasper doing something's'd've likely seen him stretching hemp should he've been let do it."

"Mr. Appleby is *very* drunk," the well dressed man asserted, indicating the would-be killer with a wave of his right hand. He had a New England accent and spoke with the carrying timbre of one well versed in addressing public meetings. Raising his voice more than was necessary just to reach the Texans and Magoon, he nevertheless gave no other indication of whether he wished everybody in the fast gathering crowd to know why the attempt upon the life of the *paria:vo* had been made. "From what he was saying inside, Ten Bears raped and killed his grandmother—!"

"Would that have been along the Trinity back in Sixty-One?" Waco suggested, rather than asked.

"He didn't say where it was," the New Englander replied, after a brief pause while daring a look redolent of suspicion at the blond youngster. "But he was clearly brooding over it and, when he saw the man responsible for the dastardly dead, the liquor must have inflamed his desire for revenge."

"There's *some* might say such was like' to happen," Waco drawled, almost mildly it seemed. "Did *you* know what he aimed to do?"

"Of course *not!*" the New Englander snorted. "If I had, naturally I would have tried to dissuade him from even trying. He isn't even a member of my par—!"

"Make way there!" barked an authoritative voice, before any more could be said. "Let me through, you men!"

Turning his gaze from the kneeling man, the blond youngster saw the soldiers who had been attracted by the shot were parting hurriedly in response to what was clearly a command. Striding through the gap was a tall, slimly built figure clad in an immaculate cavalry officer's uniform. Handsome, but with lines suggestive of a harsh and bitter nature on his clean shaven bronzed features, his dark hair was turning grey at the temples. Looking to be in his mid-forties, the "bars" on his epaulettes indicated his rank was captain. He was approaching with a rigidly square shouldered, foot stamping gait closer to marching in review than merely walking.

"What's going on here?" the officer barked, bringing himself to a heel clicking halt more usually seen in long established "crack" European regiments than the United States' Cavalry and slapping white gauntlet covered hands on his shining black weapon belt with its high riding, closed top holster at the right side for the twist hand draw favoured by his branch of the service.

"I'm afraid Mr. Appleby there responded to a drunken impulse, Captain Massey," the New Englander supplied, although the question had clearly been directed at Magoon as the senior cavalry soldier in sight. "He'd been drinking rather more than was wise and—!"

"He tried to gun down Chief Ten Bears, sir!" the sergeant major interrupted, having stiffened into a brace and brought up his right hand in an exceptionally smart salute. "Waco stopped him afore he could do it, though!"

"And just who might 'Waco' be?" Captain Barton Massey demanded of the burly non-com, having darted what appeared to be a dismissive glance at the blond youngster.

"He's one of the men sent here by General Hardin, sir," Magoon explained, in a neutral tone which nevertheless told Waco much about his feelings with regards to the officer he was addressing. "They've just now got here and, in accordance with orders from General Handiman, I was taking them to see him."

"Then, *Sergeant Major,* I would *suggest* you take *Mister* Hardin's men to see the General in accordance with his orders!" Massey stated coldly. The emphasis he had laid upon the burly Irishman's rank suggested it did not meet with his approval any more than did referring to Ole Devil Hardin by a honorific resulting from service with the Army of the Confederate States. "I'll attend to things here."

"Yo!" Magoon assented, darting a warning look at Waco before delivering another smart salute. "Would you be coming along with me now, *gentlemen*?"

"Who-all's that bow-necked son-of-a-bitch, Paddy?" the blond youngster inquired, as he and Doc were accompanying the sergeant major away from the post sulter's building.

"Brevet Colonel Barton Massey's how he's listed on the records," Magoon replied and nodded to where a young second lieutenant who had clearly been running fast was escorting Ten Bears in the opposite direction. "I'm thinking Mr. Coolin's going to have more than a little explaining to do about why he was letting the chief roam about on his lonesome."

"Is he usually that *loco*?" Waco inquired, glancing in the same direction.

"Well, he's not the *brightest* shavetail I've ever come across," the sergeant major admitted. "But I'd've thought he was just about smart enough to follow orders, 'specially when they was given by General Handiman his-own self."

"What's this 'brevet colonel' brand?" Doc asked, looking over his shoulder to where Massey was speaking with the well dressed New Englander. "I've never heard of such and, from what I know about you soldiers, he's only wearing a captain's bars."

"That's what he's wearing now, all right," Magoon replied. "But he was one of them's wound up as colonels in the War. Only, with peace cutting down the size of the Army, there wasn't enough posts for all of them. So the

War Department let them's wanted stay on, calling them 'brevet colonels', even though they only get paid for whatever rank they wound up with."

"I've heard tell there's some of 'em don't take too kind to having that 'brevet' brand," Waco commented, having heard the matter discussed by the other members of the floating outfit. "How does he feel about it?"

"He's never told me nothing, but the word is he allows a man's only entitled to the rank he gets paid for and insists on being called 'captain,' not 'colonel'," the sergeant major replied. "'Course, he could've got to thinking that way through having come here after serving five years as a military attache, or some such, over in Europe. Brought back a whole heap of notions of how things are done in regiments over there, *some* of which make good sense."

"He can't be *all* bad," Doc claimed, concluding that the non-com did not approve of the various ideas acquired in Europe by the captain. "Chasing us off the way he did, this's one time a jasper's got hurt in a shooting scrape with me around and I *didn't* wind up having to 'tend to him."

"Under the circumstances, I'm not sorry you handled things the way you did," General Philo Handiman declared, nodding with obvious approval as he looked at Waco. "If Chief Ten Bears had been shot down in cold blood, that would have ended all hope of having the *Kweharehnuh* move out of the Palo Duro country peacefully. But it was better, out of consideration of how some members of the white community would react to the news, that the man trying to do it wasn't killed."

"I fully concur with you on that, General," Senator Oswald P. Barran stated. His Southern drawl was somewhat nasal in timbre and seemed to match his invariably solemn demeanour and sombre attire. "And I'd like to add my congratulations to you for making such a good shot young man."

"Why thank you, sir," the blond cowhand replied, noticing that Captain Massey did not appear to share the approbation for his actions. Deciding against admitting he had reached a similar conclusion to that of Handiman whilst raising his Winchester to prevent the killing of the *paria:vo*, he went on, "Only I wouldn't want you-all to be thinking's I was aiming just to knock the gun out of that jasper's hand when I cut loose. Fact being, I was figuring on hitting him in the leg."

"I didn't for a moment think you were trying to *kill* him," the General asserted with a smile. Tall, well built, grey-haired and distinguished looking, clad in the dark blue double breasted frock coat and trousers which were the "undress" uniform for his rank, he nevertheless looked more like a successful and benevolent businessman than the head of the United States' Secret Service. "If you had, he'd be dead now instead of just being taken into town to have the doctor there fix his broken triggerfinger."

On reaching the regimental offices, Sergeant Major Magoon was unable to inquire after the whereabouts of Handiman immediately. First, he had had to inform his colonel about the reason for the excitement outside the post sutler's building. Regardless of how Massey might consider the affair, the commanding officer of Fort Sorrel had declared that Waco's prompt action was correct and praiseworthy. Then, learning why the burly non-com and the Texans had arrived, he told them they would find the General at the treaty cabin—as the structure was already known in the vicinity—with Senator Barran. Going to the adobe cabin, the trio had been admitted in time to hear the Captain concluding his report of the averted murder attempt.

Despite having been erected as the site for a meeting of considerable importance, due to the limited time available,

the treaty cabin was neither an elaborate nor luxurious
structure. It comprised just one room, admittance being
gained through a single door. The windows in the other
three walls had no glass panes, but curtains hung over the
inside of each to offer a measure of privacy for the occupants. Being otherwise open, as benches were provided to
seat at least twenty spectators in addition to those actively
participating, this would produce a needed means of venti-
lation. Facing the door, there was a small platform with a
table and half a dozen chairs for use by the dignitaries
during the discussions which—it was hoped—would lead
to the signing of an agreement to have the *Kweharehnuh*
Comanche leave their present domain voluntarily.

"Why did you have to send him into town just for that?"
Doc Leroy inquired, his interest in medical matters aroused
by the information just received. "I thought every fort has
its own doctor."

"So they do," Handiman confirmed. "However, the post
surgeon has been sent out with a Company on a routine
training patrol."

"*Regulations* require that he and his medical staff un-
dergo such training at regular intervals, sir!" Massey put
in, his manner icily polite and suggesting the matter had
been already raised. "So, as I found out this had not been
done recently, I had made the arrangements before this
business came up and saw no reason to cancel the order. I
couldn't foresee—!"

"I *know*, Col—Captain," the General interrupted, but in
a placatory fashion. "And his absence is in no way a reflection upon you as adjutant of this post. Rather it does
you *credit*. Such details of routine tend to be overlooked by
regiments in the field, I've heard. You'll have everything
ready for the discussions and, possibly, signing of the
treaty tonight?"

"I will, sir," Massey promised, sounding just a trifle mollified.

"I trust Captain Fog and the rest of the floating outfit will be here shortly?" Handiman inquired, turning his gaze back to the blond youngster.

"I wouldn't know whether they will or not, sir," Waco admitted. "Doc and me came here from Clinton like the telegraph message I got from Dusty said. We was expecting to find him and the boys waiting for us."

"They *aren't!*" the General claimed. "Blast it. I particularly wanted the Ysabel Kid on hand to act as interpreter."

"Ten Bears speaks reasonable English, sir," Massey pointed out. "And Civilian Scout Spelman can get by in Comanche, I've been told."

"I wanted a man present who can more than just *get by*," Handiman growled. "All too often in the past, when Indians have gone against the terms of a treaty, the chiefs responsible for it have claimed they didn't fully understand what they were told concerning the points which had been broken. This time, I wanted a man who is completely fluent in Comanche and the Kid was raised speaking it."

"Can't you hang on until he gets here?" Waco asked.

"I'm afraid not," Barran declared, before the General could speak, "This whole affair has aroused so much speculation and controversy throughout the whole country that the Governor has instructed me to bring it to a conclusion as quickly as possible. Every day we delay increases the chance of something going wrong, so I must insist upon the meeting being held tonight whether Captain Fog and his man arrive or not."

"Then that is how it will have to be," the General assented, albeit with reluctance. "You can announce that the meeting will commence at eight o'clock this evening, Captain Massey, and I want all spectators seated by seven forty-five."

"Yo!" the adjutant responded.

Concluding the building would require illumination with the meeting taking place after sundown, Waco glanced at the ceiling. He discovered lighting would be supplied by a single lamp. This was suspended in the centre from a hook, by a cord which passed over other hooks and was fastened to a peg by the window in the left side wall. Curving above the lamp was a fair-sized and saucer shaped sheet of brightly polished tin.

"That's a little notion I picked up in England," Massey commented, seeing the blond youngster exchange a quick glance with Doc Leroy who had conducted a similar scrutiny. "The sheet of tin catches and reflects the glare, giving as much light as would three ordinary lamps except there are less fumes and heat from it."

"Which will be advantageous tonight," Barren claimed. "The room will be warm enough with so many people in it without having anything to make it warmer."

"You know something, Paddy?" the slender cowhand drawled, as he, Waco and Magoon were walking away from the treaty cabin at the conclusion of their meeting with Handiman. "That bow-necked Captain of yours didn't need to go all the way to England to find such a fancy notion for lighting her up. Sam Snenton up to Dodge had his lamps fixed up that way last time the Wedge was up there."

"Only Sam doesn't have 'em that way no more," the blond corrected, remembering the reason that the lamps equipped in such a fashion which had been given to the floating outfit by the owner of the Texas House in Dodge City, Kansas, were no longer used. "But don't you go spoiling it for that nice ole Captain, 'specially after him having the goodness of heart to talk civil to common folks like you 'n' me."

• • •

Although Dusty Fog, Mark Counter and the Ysabel Kid still had not put in an appearance, Waco and Doc Leroy aided by the connivance of Sergeant Major Magoon, were already in the treaty cabin when the first of the other authorized spectators began to enter at seven forty-five in the evening.

Extending an invitation for the two young cowhands to attend, even if their companions from the OD Connected ranch had not arrived, General Handiman had told the burly non-com to escort them to their temporary accommodation and make them comfortable. Taking them to his quarters, Magoon had left them there while going to make inquiries about a matter which had aroused Waco's curiosity. He had discovered that, without having consulted the commanding officer or the General, Captain Massey had decided against arresting and holding the would be killer of Chief Ten Bears in the guardhouse of the Fort. However, as they too had felt it was advisable to try and avoid the news of the incident assuming added importance, his actions had met with the approval of his superiors. Before being sent from the post, Wilfred Appleby had been warned that he would be arrested and tried for attempted murder if he should tell anybody how he had been injured.

Despite having preceded everybody else into the building, the Texans did not appear to be making the most of their opportunity. Instead of taking their pick of the available seats, they were lounging with their backs to the wall at the right side of the door. Having been informed they must do so, they had left their gunbelts with the rest of their belongings at Magoon's quarters.

The first of the spectators to be officially granted admission were several of the Fort's officers. In accordance with the orders issued by Massey in his capacity as adjutant, all were wearing full dress uniforms with sashes but no weapon belts. With the Army personnel seated in order of seniority, the civilians invited to attend were allowed to enter. They were a variegated group. The majority were reporters from newspapers in Texas and other parts of the country. Some were native born Texans, interested in developments which could affect the lives of themselves, their families and neighbours. The rest came from outside the State, but were concerned with the possibility of speculation in land should the Palo Duro country be thrown open for white settlement. Among these was the well dressed New Englander who had spoken in Appleby's defense outside the post sutler's building. His name, Magoon had learned, was Alexander Bremont and he was an attorney for an Eastern syndicate involved in the cattle business. Studying them all with skilled gaze as they were going by, the Texans felt certain that none of them were carrying firearms concealed on their persons.

Accompanied by Chief Ten Bears, now clad in the full regalia befitting his status as *paria:vo* of the *Kweharehnuh* Comanche band, Handiman led the negotiating delegation towards the platform facing the door. Like the other officers, he and the colonel in command of Fort Sorrel were wearing their best uniform. Even the short and grizzled civilian scout at Senator Barran's side looked unusually neat and tidy, albeit a trifle uneasy over being prohibited from carrying his weapons. Bringing up the rear and closing the door behind him, Massey had on his weapon belt —with a handgun in its closed to holster—to indicate that he was responsible for the meeting taking place in good order. Although he darted a puzzled and scowling glance at the two Texans, he did not address them. Instead, as the delegation took their seats at the table, he started to walk slowly around the side of the cabin scrutinizing the spectators as if wishing to satisfy himself that none of them were armed.

"Good evening, gentlemen," Barran greeted, opening

out the roll of stiff paper which he was carrying to display the printed message and official seal it bore. "You all know why we are gathered here and I don't need to waste time explaining. However, I will read aloud the terms of the treaty for your benefit. Mr. Spelman will translate anything Chief Ten Bears cannot understand into Comanche. Then, provided he is agreeable, the chief will sign in behalf of his people and I for the United States."

There was a silence which could almost be felt throughout the room as the Senator began to read. However, listening to the elderly civilian scout translating some of the points for the benefit of the chief, Waco concluded he was far from as fluent as the Ysabel Kid would have been in employing the Comanche tongue. Nevertheless, it was also obvious that Ten Bears understood sufficient English to render the use of such an interpreter unnecessary. On being asked by Barran, he stated he was satisfied with the terms and was told to make his mark in the place being indicated.

The attention of everybody in the cabin was fixed upon the elderly *paria:vo* as he accepted the pen, holding it more like a knife than an implement with which to write. It was, the delegation and spectators all appreciated, a moment of considerable importance in the history of the State of Texas. Once Ten Bears had made his mark and Barran had signed for the United States of America, the way was open for the *Kweharehnuh* to leave the Palo Duro peacefully and without the need for coercion by the Army, almost certainly at the cost of many lives.

Just as the *paria:vo* was moving the pen clumsily towards the point on the paper indicated by the Senator's index finger, everything went black!

Until that moment, the lamp had been fully justifying the faith Massey had placed in it. Reflected by the shining saucer of tin above it, its light had bathed every corner of the cabin as effectively as would three or four lanterns without the modification. Then, without there being any apparent reason, it went out. Instantly, the room was thrown into a darkness made even more intense because every man present was taken unawares.

Nevertheless, clearly somebody either expected the sudden loss of light or was making the most of the opportunity it presented!

A firearm began to crash from about the centre of the left side wall!

Shot after shot rolled out in rapid succession!

The red spurts of the muzzle blasts were lancing in the direction of the platform!

Audible even through the commotion being caused by the alarmed occupants of the cabin, there was a clacking noise between each detonation. It was the distinctive sound made by a lever action mechanism, such as was fitted to the products of the Winchester Repeating Arms Company, being put through its reloading cycle to throw out an empty cartridge case and replenish the chamber with a loaded bullet from the tubular magazine beneath the barrel while also cocking the hammer.

Pandemonium reigned in the room!

The pitch blackness seemed to be rendered even more intense by the fiery glow which erupted each time the weapon was fired!

Men were shouting profanities as they dropped to the floor, overturning the benches upon which they were sitting and trying to get out of the possible line of fire!

However, spurred by a cry of pain and the heavy thud of a body falling from the direction of the platform, two of the occupants retained something of their usual presence of mind!

"I'll go look, Doc!" Waco snapped, finding the handle and starting to throw open the door. "You'll be needed in here!"

"Sounds that way!" the slender cowhand admitted. "But don't forget you're not tot—!"

Before the warning could be completed, the young blond sprang from the all pervading gloom of the cabin into the somewhat lesser darkness of the open air. Ignoring the shouts which were ringing out all around, but instinctively continuing to count the shots as he was running, he set his right hand into motion with the speed of long training. Instead of closing around the staghorn handle of the Colt Artillery Model Peacemaker which would normally have hung at the point, his reaching fingers encountered only the material of the Levi's leg. However, there was no time for him to curse the orders which had caused him to attend the meeting unarmed. Already he was starting to turn the corner beyond which eight shots had been fired. The sounds interspersing the shots suggested a Winchester was being used. Even if this was a carbine and not a rifle, the man responsible could still have five more bullets at his disposal.

Arriving at that far from comforting conclusion, Waco could not prevent himself from passing around the end of the building with empty hands!

Ready to stake everything upon a rolling dive, which hopefully would carry him under the barrel of whatever type of Winchester was being used before it could be swung into alignment upon him, the youngster discovered that the desperate gamble would not be required. For all that, he found himself more mystified than relieved. The last of the eight shots had been discharged an instant before he came around the corner, but the wall along which he was gazing was completely deserted.

There was no sign of the shooter, nor even a sound to suggest he was already running away from the building!

Skidding to a halt, Waco was utterly baffled by the discovery. It was something he could not have foreseen, or even suspected might happen. On turning the corner, he had expected and been ready to find himself up against a desperate man armed with some kind of Winchester or perhaps its predecessor, the Henry rifle. Yet the eventuality had not materialized. There was nothing of the sort awaiting him. Just a bare wall. No armed assailant. No one taking flight. It was a set of circumstances which the youngster found himself unable to explain.

Standing and scratching his head in puzzlement, but coming no closer to a solution to the mystery, Waco gazed about him without seeing or hearing the slightest trace of the man with the repeater. That nobody else was close by came as no surprise. In accordance with the orders given by Massey, only the delegates and invited spectators were permitted to approach the building. Even Magoon had gone away after having allowed the blond and Doc to enter. However, attracted by the disturbance, the occupants of various buildings were now running to investigate. Most were holding weapons and several carried lanterns.

Suddenly, Waco realized his life was not only in danger from the inexplicably absent shooter.

Any of the approaching soldiers, seeing a figure erupting from, or running around the cabin might assume he was the fleeing perpetrator of the disturbance and open fire upon him without waiting to make an identification!

"It's Waco, Paddy!" the youngster yelled, pleased to see the burly sergeant major was in the forefront of the men coming towards him and was carrying a bull's-eye lantern. "General Handiman'd not be wanting folks crowding around the cabin!"

"Everybody stop right where you are!" Magoon commanded in a booming bellow. Such was the respect he had established for his authority, the enlisted men—no officers had reached the scene as yet having a greater distance to traverse—obeyed instantly. Walking forward, he went on in a lower tone, "What's happened?"

"Somebody started throwing lead through the window there," Waco explained, thinking fast. "What I heard, somebody on the platform got hit. Send one of your fellers to fetch Doc's black bag and lend me your lantern, *amigo*. You'd best have a couple more sent inside and, was I you, I'd get the rest of these fellers looking for the jasper who did the shooting. Only tell them to go careful. Unless he's tossed it away, which isn't a whole heap likely, he's toting a Winchester and it'll have some bullets in it even happen he hasn't had time to do any reloading."

"Which way'd he go?" Magoon asked, after accepting the first two suggestions he had received. He was quite willing to keep on taking the advice of a civilian much younger than himself.

"I'm damned if I know, or how the hell he did go, the son-of-a-bitch," Waco admitted, accepting the lantern from the sergeant major and watching two more being taken into the cabin. "But somehow he was out of sight *afore* I could get from the door to the corner and I couldn't even hear him lighting a shuck from the window."

"Spread out and start looking for anybody carrying a repeater of any kind, or who looks to have been running!" Magoon ordered, not waiting for the officers he saw approaching to arrive and assume command. "Only watch how you go up against him, he might not take kind to the notion of being fetched back. Here, corpsman, get inside. There's at least one wounded man needing 'tending."

"I'm not a qualified doctor!" protested the soldier wearing a long white coat, to whom the last words were directed.

"You don't need to tell me that," the sergeant major replied. "But there's a feller inside's is!"

"Thank the Lord for that!" the medical corpsman gasped and hurried towards the cabin.

"I'll say amen to it!" Magoon asserted, then noticed what the young Texan was doing with the lantern. "It's too hard underfoot for you to be reading sign, good's the Kid's taught you to be."

"Way too hard," the blond agreed, without halting his search of the ground around the left side window. His tone was pensive as he returned the lantern and continued, "There's nary a smidgin of sign around here—Or *anything* else, comes to that!"

Instead of elaborating upon the final cryptic utterance, Waco led the way around the treaty cabin. On entering, he found some semblance of order had been restored since the arrival of illumination. Before telling Doc—who was still standing by the door—of the arrangements he had made, the youngster gazed around. Despite everybody in between having regained their feet, he was able to see the platform. What he saw on the dais was far from comforting.

As had been suggested by the muzzle flashes, the delegation were the target for the man with the repeater. Clearly some of his bullets had taken effect despite being fired in conditions far from conducive to accuracy. Blood was dribbling from a shallow nick on General Handiman's left cheek. Having had an even more fortunate escape, Senator Barran was staring as if mesmerized at a gash in the right sleeve of his jacket. It seemed that none of the other white men had been touched. However, Chief Ten Bears was slumped unmoving in a partially sitting position against the wall. Blood was running from holes in his left shoulder and the right side of his chest.

"Paddy's sent for your bag!" Waco told his companion.

"*Bueno!*" Doc replied, nodding in gratitude to the burly non-com who had entered after reporting to the senior of the newly arrived officers what had happened and was being done. "Now can you get me through to the platform, *amigo*?"

"Make way there now, *gentlemen*!" Magoon thundered, drowning the babble of excited conversation. "Will you be letting the doctor here through, *please*!"

"*Doctor?*" Captain Massey barked in the silence which followed the words of the burly non-com. He had contrived to reach but not yet step on to the platform. Glaring in puzzlement at the two Texans who were following the pale and clearly worried corpsman through the gap which had opened in the crowd, the captain went on, "Where the hell is the *doctor*, Magoon?"

"Right here," Doc introduced, pointing a thumb at his chest.

"*You?*" the adjutant snorted. "If this is some kind of jo—!"

"It *isn't*, Captain!" Handiman stated emphatically. "Thank god you're here, *Doctor* Leroy. Is there anything you want?"

"I've sent for my bag," the slender cowhand replied, thankful he was known to the General in his professional —if not formally qualified—capacity and had received his backing. "But I could do with a whole heap less folks standing around."

"Clear the cabin, Captain Massey!" Handiman barked, with no more hesitation than he had shown when giving his seal of approval to the Texan. "And have everybody searched as they go out!"

"They were all searched and, where necessary, made to leave behind any weapons they were carrying before they were allowed inside, sir," the adjutant pointed out, with the deference of one who was questioning an order given by a clearly furious senior officer. "And, judging from the clicking sound I heard between the shots, I'd say it was a repeating rifle and not a revolver being used."

"That's the way I heard it, General," the civilian scout seconded. "Whoever did it must've cut loose through the window with a repeater, not a handgun."

"I heard the lever working, sir," the Colonel supported.

"Very well, don't bother searching them," Handiman rescinded, also having heard the distinctive sound but, in his anxiety not giving a thought to its meaning until the matter was brought to his attention. "Clear the room and then I want some questions answered."

"Hey, *amigo*," Waco called, as Massey turned a coldly pointed look in his direction. "I reckon you'll likely be needing me, won't you?"

"Best stick around in case I do," Doc confirmed, taking the hint. Stepping on to the platform, he continued over his shoulder, "Anyways, the General's going to want to be told what you found outside."

"I certainly am," Handiman agreed, dabbing at his cheek with a handkerchief. Seeing the slender cowhand glancing his way, he continued, "Don't worry about me. See to the Chief, he needs it more than I do."

"I'll have the corpsman 'tend to you soon's my bag's here," Doc promised, without saying it had been his intention to look after the wounded Indian first.

"Shall I have everybody wait at the post sutler's, sir?" Massey asked, watching the Texans going towards Ten Bears.

"Send somebody else to take them there," Handiman instructed. "Stay here yourself and, as soon as they've gone, find out why that god-damned lamp of yours failed."

For a moment, it seemed the adjutant meant to make a comment of some sort. Then the discipline instilled by years of military training caused him merely to stiffen to a brace and reply, "Yo!" in a neutral tone which nevertheless sounded just a trifle sullen.

If the General noticed the inflexion in the Captain's voice, he made no reference to it. Instead, he turned his attention to where Doc had commenced an examination of the wounded man and asked, "Is he still alive?"

"Yes," the slender cowhand replied, having eased the torso of the sitting man forward to look at his back. "His head cracked against the wall as he was going down. It knocked him unconscious and I hope he stays that way for a while."

"Why?" Handiman inquired.

"The bullets are still in him," Doc explained. "And they're going to have to come out to keep him alive."

"They're *both* still inside him?" Waco queried, looking away from the platform.

"Both of them," Doc confirmed and his gaze also flickered briefly to the window at the left side of the room. Then, having exchanged a quick glance with the blond youngster, his voice took on a note of asperity as he went on, "I hope whoever's fetching my bag's not taking the long trail there and back!'

"Here it is now!" the commanding officer of the Fort announced in a relieved tone, as a breathless soldier entered and hurried forward.

"Do you have *everything* in there, *amigo*?" Waco inquired, watching the slender cowhand accept the black bag which he had carried strapped to the horn of his saddle.

"Why sure," Doc drawled, having looked around on noticing the emphasis placed upon one word and drawn the correct conclusion from the way in which the blond youngster's right hand lifted in what seemed to be a casual gesture. Its forefinger was slightly crooked, the other three more bent and the thumb curved above them in a fashion which he found significant. "I *always* have *everything* in here, just like pappy taught me."

"*Bueno!*" Waco declared, lowering and relaxing the

hand without anybody except the other Texan drawing conclusions from what he had said and done. "You never know
when you might be needing *it*!"

"It's ready if I do," the slender cowhand promised, then
his voice took on a brusque tone and he continued, "Now
I'd be *obliged* should the platform be cleared."

"Well, Captain Massey," Handiman said, after everybody except Doc and the corpsman had stepped to the floor
of the cabin. "Why did it go out?"

"I don't know, sir," the adjutant admitted, having lowered and examined the lamp which failed at such an inop-
portune moment. "There's still plenty of oil in it and the
wick hasn't burned away."

"Sam Snenton, up to Dodge City, used to light the Texas
House with lamps fitted that way," Waco remarked. "Only
he quit 'cause the trail hands learned you could put 'em out
by giving the rope they was hung from a jerk."

"Then the man with the rifle must have reached in and
done it!" Barran guessed. "Or he had an accomplice with
him to do it."

"Did I hear that you went out after the man doing the
shooting, Waco?" the General inquired.

"Yes, sir," the youngster answered. "Only, when I got
'round to the window, there wasn't hide nor hair of him to
be seen."

"You mean he'd already run away?" Barran suggested.

"If there was anybody out there in the first place," Waco
replied.

"How do you mean, 'If there was anybody out there'?"
Massey barked derisively, putting down the lamp and wav-
ing his left hand towards where Doc was kneeling by Ten
Bears. "Are you saying we all just *imagined* the shooting?"

"Nope," the youngster answered. "I'm saying it might
not've been done from *outside*."

"What makes you think *that*?" Handiman asked, remembering what Ole Devil Hardin had told him about the blond's flair for deductive reasoning.

"I was going 'round the corner as the last shot was fired," Waco explained, concealing a slight nervousness at finding himself being studied by so many older men. "Only there wasn't anybody in sight when I turned it."

"He'd already run away," Massey stated.

"He *could* have," the blond conceded. "Only he wouldn't't've had time to pick up all the empty shells and there wasn't even one lying out there. Which there *should* have been, happen he was using either a Winchester or a Henry like it sounded."

"It had to be one or the other," the adjutant asserted. "We all heard the lever action being operated and he fired about a dozen shots."

"Only *eight*," Waco corrected. "I counted 'em *real* careful, figuring I'd be going up against him."

"Very well, only *eight*," Massey accepted, but with obvious disdain. "That still means he must have been using a rifle, or at least a carbine. I've never seen a *revolver* chamberred for *eight* shots. Have you?"

"Not just for eight, but I've seen one's was made to hold ten," the blond answered. "General Hardin's got one hell of a good collection of handguns hanging in his study and I've been let spend a fair amount of time looking 'em over. One of 'em's a pin-fire ten-shooter's was made some place in Europe and got sent over here to be sold to the Confederate States' Army. What I was told about it and its mates, they wasn't popular. Seems they was reckoned too big, heavy 'n' delicate, on top of it being nigh on impossible to get a regular supply of bullets for 'em."

"I know the type of revolver you mean," Handiman supported, also having studied the collection when visiting the OD Connected ranch. "But, although I've never seen it fired, I wouldn't think it would sound like a lever action mechanism when it's being cocked."

"Even if it did sound that way," Massey went on, with the air of producing an irrefutable argument. "Everybody was searched before they were allowed to come here. It was impossible for anybody to have brought in a revolver, particularly one as large as you say that European ten-shooter was."

"One feller brought a gun in with him, though," Waco contradicted.

"God damn your impertinence!" the adjutant snarled, seeing all the other men were looking in the same direction as the blond youngster. His right hand slapped on to the closed flap of the holster attached to his weapon belt and he continued just as heatedly. "Of course I'm wearing a *revolver*—!"

"And I'm betting those fellers from the newspapers remember you are," Waco drawled, having drawn certain conclusions and now seeking a way of putting them to the test. "Which they could start asking questions when it comes out that Ten Bears might not've been shot by a rifle from *outside* the treaty cabin."

"How dare you imply—?" Massey began, his face dark with anger.

"He has a point, Captain!" Handiman put in, deciding something far more serious than idle curiosity or a desire to embarass the adjutant had prompted the blond youngster's comment. "Show us your revolver, please!"

"I agree with you, General!" Barran declared, then turned an apologetic glance towards Massey. "Considering the circumstances, we must make certain there can't be the slightest reason for suspicion, or even doubt, where *any-body* connected with this unfortunate business is concerned."

"I *protest*, sir!" the adjutant growled, stiffening into a

brace and throwing a look at the commanding officer of the Fort as if seeking support.

"Your protest is noted, Captain Massey," Handiman asserted, giving the Colonel no chance to speak. "But I'm still *ordering* you to show us your sidearm, so we can check it hasn't been fired."

"As you wish, sir!" the adjutant answered, his tone neutral. "Here it is!"

Watching Massey walk towards the older men, opening the flap of the holster, Waco felt uneasy. Except for the objections which were understandable for one of his background when placed in an embarrassing position by somebody he considered a social inferior, he was showing no trace of alarm over what he had been ordered to do. This could be due to having a clear conscience. In which case, the theory which had led the youngster to make the suggestion was wrong and, at the very least, he would be required to tender an apology to the adjutant.

Continuing to advance with the brisk and drill-like precision which characterized all his movements, turning the palm of his right hand outwards, Massey brought the sidearm from its holster. However, despite having a butt shaped in a similar fashion, it was not any kind of revolver. Instead of having a rotating cylinder to hold its bullets, there was a tubular magazine such as was fitted to Winchester repeating rifles and carbines beneath the barrel. To further emphasize the resemblance, the triggerguard was made in the form of a ringed lever.

Although Waco had had his supposition confirmed by the firearm which was brought into view, having remembered examining and firing one from Ole Devil Hardin's collection, he was not given time to say so!

The young blond was not alone in making the identification!

"A Volcanic pistol!" Handiman ejaculated, then noticed

and realized the significance of the hammer being in the fully cocked position. There could be only one reason why a man with Massey's knowledge of firearms would have holstered the weapon in such a potentially unsafe condition. "Then i—!"

Before the General could complete the accusation, the adjutant lunged to catch Barran by the left arm and, thrusting the muzzle of the Volcanic pistol against his side, pulled him until they were standing well clear of the others.

"Don't anybody make a move!" Massey demanded.

"What in h—?" the Colonel began and seemed on the point of stepping forward.

"Stand still, damn you!" the adjutant warned, gouging the muzzle deeper into the politician's side. "Or I'll put a bullet through his guts and, doctor or no doctor on hand, he'll die in agony!"

"Do as he says, *everybody*!" Handiman ordered and, having given considerable thought to how such a situation might be coped with, acted upon his conclusion that the best way would be to play for time. "Why on earth did you shoot Chief Ten Bears, Captain?"

"Do you really need me to answer *that*?" the adjutant challenged derisively, glancing towards the platform where Doc Leroy was kneeling alongside the unmoving Indian. Although he had not yet taken anything out of his black bag, he had it fully open.

"Certainly I do," Handiman replied. "The Chief was ready to bring his people out of the Palo Duro peacefully, instead of the Army being sent to fetch them."

"And that's why I did it!" Massey asserted. "I commanded a regiment with distinction in the War and was about to be promoted to General with my own Brigade when those goddamned Rebs gave up and peace came. Then, instead of the advancement I'd *earned*, I was fobbed off with an *unpaid* brevet rank and sent to Europe as a Captain. When I was brought back, in spite of having *carried* the Military Attache all the time I was there, I was assigned as adjutant to this son-of-a-bitching, dead-or-alive, stinking mud-hole."

"I told you that was only temporary!" the Colonel protested. "You'd have had command of Company 'A' and been my second-in-command by the end of the month!"

"And spent the rest of my career rotting away out here where nobody would ever hear about me!" Massey went on bitterly.

"Unless you were given the chance to distinguish yourself in a campaign to force the *Kweharehnuh* out of the Palo Duro," Handiman continued. "But Ten Bears coming to make peace was going to stop the necessity for that. So you decided to make sure he didn't sign the treaty."

"That's how it was," Massey confirmed, darting a glance filled with hatred at Waco. "I saw my chance and took it."

"But it hasn't worked," the General answered. "You've only wounded Ten Bears and, from all I've heard about Doctor Leroy there, he'll live."

"I'd be willing to bet on it," the slender cowhand declared, with complete confidence, his right hand resting on the open top of the bag.

"And I'm willing to bet the Chief will still be agreeable to signing the treaty," Handiman supplemented, hoping he sounded as assured as the kneeling Texan. "So you might as well surrender. You can't get away."

"The hell I can't!" the adjutant denied. "Just as a precaution, I've two good horses saddled and loaded with all I'll need, under the pretense that I was expecting to be sent with dispatches when the meeting ended. You're going to pass orders for them to be waiting for me at the main gate and I'm to be let go. You'll also say that everybody has to stay indoors until after I've gone."

"Why would I do that?" the General inquired, although he could guess the answer.

"Because you don't want that damned red-stick to learn he was shot by one of the Army officers assigned to guard him," Massey replied. "If he hears that, he'll not be likely to sign your god-damned peace treaty."

"We could keep him from finding out," Handiman countered, despite conceding there was some justification in the assumption. "I can count on everybody in here to keep quiet—!"

"You couldn't explain away having the Senator here gutshot," Massey denied. "There are men around the Fort who'll be only too eager to let that red-stick bastard know what happened and claim it proves the Army doesn't want his people to come out peacefully. So I'm taking Barran with me as a hostage and the only way you can keep him alive is by letting me go. You can announce I've taken him to make a report about what happened. Do as I say and you'll at least have a chance of preventing anybody from learning the truth. Try any tricks and I'll kill him, then take my chances on getting away."

"Aw hell, General!" Waco put in loudly. "That bow-necked Yankee son-of-a-bitch's only *bluffing*. Afore he can start gut-shooting the Senator, he's going to have to reload that fancy handgun."

"*Reload?*" the General queried, noticing a change had come to the demeanour and tone of the blond youngster.

"Why sure," Waco asserted, his manner and voice redolent of smug self satisfaction at having reached a conclusion which had eluded older and more experienced men. He made it clear that he was particularly pleased to consider he had got the better of Massey as he continued, "*General* Hardin's got him a couple of them Volcanic guns, which how I figured out one'd been used 'n' not a Winchester. Thing being, that gun only holds *eight* of them itty-bitty bullets with the powder and cap inside 'em, 'stead of having a regular cartridge case. And, seeing's how ole bow-neck there's already shot off *eight* to put just two into the chief—!"

"Don't even *think* of it!" Massey spat out, seeing the Colonel and the General's aide-de-camp stiffen as if contemplating rushing him. "That beef-head son-of-a-bitch isn't as smart as he *imagines* and he's made a *very* bad mistake. It was a six inch barrelled Volcanic he used and that only takes eight balls, but *this* of mine is the eight inch barrel model and holds *ten* when fully charged, which it was when I came in here."

"I'm not from Missouri!" Waco snorted derisively. "But I've still got to be *showed* you ain't empty!"

"You'll be more than just 'showed' if you take a step this way, you smart-assed son-of-a-bitch!" the adjutant threatened, as the other officers froze into immobility on receiving a prohibitive glare from Handiman. "I can cut you down and have the gun back against Barran's ribs with the last ball for him before anybody else can reach me. They're not armed to get me from where they stand."

"*They* might not be armed," the blond youngster answered, in the manner of one playing an unsuspected trump card. "But I *never* go no place 'less 'n I'm toting iron!"

"You were searched and disarmed before you were allowed to come in!" Massey claimed, but an uneasy feeling assailed him. "I made sure of that—!"

"Only I didn't get here with the others," Waco reminded. "Paddy Magoon let me in and he didn't figure he'd need to search me when I left my gunbelt in his room. Happen he had, he'd've found I was toting a lil ole Remington stingy gun back here."

Saying the last few words, the blond youngster began to

swagger forward and reached behind his back beneath the calfskin vest with his right hand!

Further fury flooded through Massey as he appreciated the ramifications of the latest, completely unanticipated development!

Until that moment, being aware of how delicate the situation was, the adjutant had felt sure Handiman would yield to his terms rather than ruin whatever chance might remain of salvaging the treaty negotiations. Furthermore, knowing that Barran was a leading advocate of making peace with the *Kweharehnuh* and having them leave the Palo Duro of their own free will, the General would not endanger his life. However, lacking such an assessment of the affair and clearly seeking to gain added acclaim by a grandstand play, the young Texan would not be swayed by such considerations.

The thought increased the hatred which Massey had already developed for the cause of his predicament. If it had not been for the surprising knowledge of firearms possessed by the blond cowhand, even though he had failed to exchange the Volcanic for his service revolver under the pretence of escorting the spectators from the treaty cabin, it would have remained undetected. Furthermore, eager to show himself to be correct in his judgement, the brash young Texan would not hesitate before bringing out and using the weapon he had succeeded in carrying upon his person.

"Damn you!" the adjutant spat furiously, watching the blond's bent right elbow alter the direction in which it was moving and starting to swing the Volcanic away from Barran.

As soon as the Senator was no longer threatened by the unconventional weapon, the deep bellow of a heavy calibre revolver sounded. Struck in the centre of the forehead by the bullet, Massey was knocked away from his intended hostage. An involuntary reaction caused him to squeeze the trigger. However, the lead ejected through the eight inch barrel of the Volcanic flew harmlessly into the floor some feet from where Waco was standing with both hands empty.

"*Gracias*, Doc," Waco drawled, turning his gaze in the direction from which the shot which had saved him had come. "I'm right surely pleased you had *everything* in that ole bag of your'n."

"You can always count on that," the slender cowhand replied. He was still in the kneeling posture and he lowered the smoking, wooden handled Colt Artillery Model Peacemaker which he had held double handed at shoulder height and arms' length as an aid to taking a careful aim. "Pappy taught me that a doctor out here should *always* tote a six-gun in his bag. You might've got that bow-necked *hombre* to turn his pistol sooner, though. I'm wanting to start 'tending to the Chief here."

"Take my advice, young man," General Handiman requested gravely, entering the treaty cabin with his aide-de-camp about half an hour after the shooting of Captain Massey. With the exception of the Texans and corpsman, he and the others who stayed behind had left to deal with the crowd attracted by the second gun shots. On returning, he found only Waco present. "Don't *ever* let yourself be given an assignment like *mine*. I've just been *lying* fit to damn my immortal soul, supposedly explaining what happened in here."

"Well I'll be switched!" the blond youngster ejaculated. "And here's me thinking only us hired hands needed to do things like that."

"How do you mean?" Handiman inquired, looking at the now deserted stage.

"You reminded me of something I was saying to Doc's we rode in this afternoon," Waco replied. "Anyways, ole

Chief Ten Bears'll pull through. Them Volcanic bullets don't have a whole heap of power and they hadn't gone in deep enough to be dangerous's long's they was got out soon after. Getting hit unexpected by 'em caused him to fall backwards, so's his head banged the wall and knocked him unconscious. Afore he was toted back to his bedground, he told us's he's still wanting to sign the treaty."

"We have you and your friend to thank for that," the General claimed, noticing the youngster was no longer speaking and behaving in his previous arrogant cocksure manner. "And I'm going to write and tell Ole Devil so."

"Don't do *that*, sir!" Waco close to pleaded. "The rest of the boys'd rawhide me something mean happen you did."

"Very well," Handiman assented with a smile. "But I need to know how you arrived at your conclusions. I need all the facts for my confidential report, so my aide had better write everything down while its still fresh in your mind and I'll be able to raise any points you don't cover."

"Where'd you want me to start?" the youngster asked.

"From the shooting which wounded the chief," the General replied.

"Well, sir," Waco obliged. "I went out expecting to see a feller using a Winchester through the window. When he wasn't there 'n' I couldn't see nor hear him lighting a shuck and there wasn't even any empty shell cases lying around, I figured I must've just imagined hearing the lever clicking. Comes Doc saying neither bullet'd gone through Ten Bears, which they would've had even a carbine been used, I reckoned it must've been a revolver 'cepting there'd been eight shots and I couldn't bring no eight-shooter to mind, nor one's'd sound like a lever action when it was being fired. That ten-shooter came to mind, which started me thinking about Ole Devil's gun collection 'n' I remembered the Volcanics I'd seen 'n' been let use."

"Why did you suspect Captain Massey?" Handiman asked, the explanation having been brought to a temporary halt to allow his aide to write down in shorthand what had been said so far. "Did you remember seeing him near the window when the lights went out?"

"No, sir," Waco denied. "Like everybody else, I was watching Ten Bears getting ready to sign when the light went out; which's one of the things he must've been counting on."

"Then what did make you suspect him?"

"He'd had everybody else searched afore they was let in. I'd looked 'em all over as they came by me and was willing to bet none of 'em was toting a gun of any kind, much less something the length of the Volcanic. Top of that, he'd been the only one moving around once the talking started. He'd had that fancy lamp fitted and likely knowed how to put it out by jerking on its cord. Likely he hadn't thought of gunning the Chief down when he sent the doctor out with a patrol, but he'd seen how it could help. Those bullets he'd be using wasn't over powerful, but they'd be more likely to kill if there wasn't nobody hereabouts's could dig 'em out. Top of which, he was able to bring the gun in without nobody seeing anything strange about it."

"But why use the Volcanic and not an ordinary revolver?" the aide asked.

"To make everybody think the shooting was done through the window with a Winchester, not inside using a handgun," Waco explained. "I knowed he wouldn't show us his gun for me asking, General, but reckoned he'd have to was you to tell him. Trouble was, I hadn't figured to him grabbing the Senator that way."

"You found a most effective way to counter him, though," Handiman praised. "Damn it, you almost had *me* believing you were a brash young hot-head trying for a grandstand play as you did him."

"I figured acting that way'd rile him, top of him not liking me too much already, so's he'd try to gun me down. And I knowed Doc would back my play with that ole hawgleg he totes in his doctoring bag once I'd got the Volcanic turned away from the Senator."

"Why did you go to that much trouble if you were sure it wasn't loaded?" the aide wanted to know.

"I *wasn't* sure," Waco corrected. "Fact being, knowing one model was a ten shooter, I reckoned he'd still got two bullets left. So I had to make him turn his gun my way afore Doc cut loose, 'cause even head-hit he could 'n' did get off a shot."

"You took a big chance doing it," Handiman declared, then realized he was once again embarrassing the youngster and sought to bring a lighter note into the conversation. "And I'm not sorry that you were proved correct in your theory. If you hadn't been, we could have been dealing with an invisible man with an invisible Winchester."

"Yes sir," Waco agreed with a grin. "And I don't *see* how you could catch a feller like that."

PART THREE

Responsibility To Kinfolks

More than one woman, including several who were married and qualified as "good" by the standards of the Old West, directed a glance filled with admiration at Mark Counter as he was strolling along the main street of Trail End, Kansas in the afternoon sun. There was, in fact, considerable justification for the open or—depending upon the nature of the one concerned—overt scrutiny. It would have been an exceptional crowd in which he did not stand out prominently.

Three inches over six foot in height and in his mid-twenties, Mark presented a picture which Frederic Remington and many other an artist might have taken pleasure in committing to canvas. All in all, there was excellent cause for his once having been described as looking like a Grecian god of old who had exchanged the traditional flowing white robe and sandals of Mount Olympus for the attire of a cowhand from Texas. Beneath neatly barbered and curly golden blond hair, his tanned and clean shaven features were almost classically handsome. There was a tremendous spread to his shoulders, with the torso trimming to a slender waist and long, straight, powerful legs. Yet, despite weighing something over two hundred pounds, he gave no suggestion of being slow, clumsy, or awkward. Rather the opposite was the case. He moved with a springiness to his step which indicated his leisurely stride could easily be changed into very rapid motion if the need arose.

Few of those around the blond giant were as well dressed as he was, but his elegant attire was not a result of the usual habit of cowhands to fancy up their appearance with the extra money earned by working on a trail drive. Although employed as a member of the OD Connected ranch's floating outfit, which brought him a slightly higher rate of pay than that of the ordinary hands, he was also sufficiently wealthy in his own right to indulge his sartorial tastes at all times. His white J.B. Stetson hat, moulded in the style of Texans, had a brown leather band decorated by genuine silver conchas around its crown. Tightly rolled, the scarlet bandana trailing long ends over his massive chest was silk. His light blue shirt and yellowish-brown Nankeen trousers, the turned back cuffs of the legs hanging outside top quality brown high heeled and sharp toed boots with elaborate stitching, were of the best materials available and clearly tailored for him. Such an excellent fit could never have come ready made from the shelves of a store.

Regardless of how the distaff portion of the onlookers might be studying Mark, one point was being observed by practically every man he passed!

The blond giant was not wearing a gunbelt!

Nor did Mark give any indication of carrying weapons elsewhere on his person!

There were some amongst the crowd who concluded the blond giant must be a wealthy young visitor from the East and had elected to copy the clothing of cowhands, but had had the good sense not to add to the provocation his attire might cause by being armed. The majority were better informed with regards to his status, although a proportion of them wondered why a man with his reputation was not "dressed"; as cowhands from Texas claimed to be when wearing firearms. A few of those who knew the reason wondered why a man his calibre had consented to appear in public without his usual armament.

On being appointed town marshal, Stanley Woodrow Markham had elected to follow the training he had acquired as a deputy for a peace officer who had attained considerable fame and acclaim during 1870.

While serving as town marshal of Abilene when it was at the peak of its boom as the terminus of the Chisholm Trail, reversing the trend amongst other Kansas' peace officers, Thomas James "Tom" Smith had performed his duties without going around armed to the teeth. Instead, he had put his faith in impartiality, fair dealing, courage and skill as a fist fighter. Aided by a general reluctance to draw a gun upon an unarmed man, a point of view considerably influenced by the knowledge that to kill in such circumstances was likely to result in being hanged for murder, these qualities had earned him the respect of the local community and visitors alike.[1]

Remembering the success achieved by Smith, Markham had agreed to take office with the proviso that the mayor and council ratified a civic ordinance which would ban the wearing of firearms within the city limits. Asking if he considered adopting such a ruling was wise, or even possible to enforce, he had claimed there were two reasons in particular why it would work. Firstly, Tom Smith's period in office at Abilene

1. Having been appointed as a Deputy United States' Marshal for the Abilene Federal Judicial District, Thomas James "Tom" Smith was killed whilst attempting to make an arrest on November the 2nd, 1870. This was one of the few recorded occasions when he was carrying arms in the execution of his duty, but he was shot with a rifle as he was announcing his intentions and then beheaded by an accomplice of the man he was after as he fell wounded. J.T.E.

was remembered favourably in comparison with his predecessors and successor, and with the general run of peace officers for the Kansas' railroad towns. Secondly, since having been cleaned up by members of Ole Devil Hardin's floating outfit at the request of Governor Mansfield,[2] Trail End had retained the good name it had acquired as being an honest and fairly run community.

After some discussion, it had been decided to try what was to become known as the "no guns around town" ordinance for a trial period of a month. Therefore, posters had been printed and placed in prominent positions in and around the town giving warning of the changed conditions. They announced that, on arrival, every visitor was required to hand over his weapons for safe-keeping to the marshal, his deputies, the desk clerk of the hotel, owner of the rooming-house, or—if only passing through without taking accommodation—the bartender of the first saloon entered, to be collected on departure. It was also stated that the same rules applied to the citizens.

Having been informed by Markham—who was hired at his instigation—of what was intended, Governor Mansfield had seen it as offering an opportunity to change the impression created in the East that the towns of his State were so wild and dangerous only the use of armed peace officers could maintain some semblance of law and order. Equally cognizant of the difficulties which would confront the new marshal whilst enforcing an ordinance likely to prove unpopular, he had seen a way to help the situation.

Arranging to meet Dusty Fog, who was newly arrived in Mulrooney with a trail herd from the OD Connected, the Governor had explained the position. Always willing to help a friend of his uncle and knowing Ole Devil Hardin would expect him to do so, the small Texan had given his approval.

2. Told in: *The Small Texan* and *The Town Tamers*. J.T.E.

Although he could not be personally spared to put into effect the scheme he had in mind, he had declared Mark would be the ideal substitute. Hearing what was proposed and eager to avoid various social functions which he would be expected to attend by virtue of being related to Ole Devil and Dusty, another member of the floating outfit had offered to accompany the blond giant and this was accepted.

Although less sanguine in the case of Charles Henry "Red" Blaze, who had a not entirely undeserved reputation for being quick tempered and impetuous, the wisdom of Mark having been selected was apparent to Mansfield. No other member of the floating outfit, their respective individual qualifications notwithstanding, possessed his sheer physical presence. He had a well merited fame for being a tophand in all aspects of working cattle, whether on the open range or the trail. In addition, stories of his prodigious feats of strength and skill at bare-handed fighting were common knowledge throughout the West.[3] Therefore, how he reacted to the "no guns in Trail End" ordinance would be noted by every other Texan. Nor, while they would probably be less impressed by his activities in the ranching business, would his behaviour pass unnoticed by visitors who were employed in other occupations.

Travelling from Mulrooney by train, with their horses in a box car, Mark and Red had found their arrival was expected. A considerable crowd had gathered to find out what the response would be when Markham requested the blond giant to surrender his brown *buscadero* gunbelt with the brace of ivory handled Colt Cavalry Model Peacemakers in its fast draw holsters. That he had shown no hesitation before doing so, also handing over his Winchester Model of 1873 rifle from its saddleboot, had become a major talking point round

3. Details of Mark Counter's family background and special qualifications are recorded in: *Appendix Two*. J.T.E.

Trail End. From what he and his companion had overheard, the general concensus of opinion considered his willing acquiescence indicated a belief and trust in the new marshal. However, having taken into account his Herculean build and mindful of the many stories told about him, those who might otherwise have accused him of having been too frightened of Markham to refuse, had also concluded it would prove unwise and probably painful in the extreme to make the suggestion to his face.

In addition to having been told to let it be seen they were content to go along with the "no guns in Trail End" edict, Mark and Red were instructed to remain until sure the message was firmly implanted. To help achieve this, it had become the practice of the blond giant to stroll through the streets at least twice a day and allow his continued unarmed condition to be observed. He had also sought to persuade each newly arrived trail crew that they had nothing to fear from obeying the civic ordinance. Such was his standing amongst his fellow Texans that, as Governor Mansfield had hoped would prove the case, there had been neither active opposition nor unpleasantness from any of them when called upon to give up their firearms while within the city limits.

Six days had elapsed since the two members of the floating outfit reached Trail End. Satisfied they had done all that was required of them, Mark was taking what he had decided would be his final afternoon perambulation. As they would be leaving in the morning, it was his intention to invite a few friends from the period when he had served as a deputy town marshal to have dinner with him and Red that evening. One of the invited guests had purchased the Educated Thirst Saloon after the not undeserved death of the previous, far from honest, owner. As he had known the impact would be greater, he had taken his strolls alone and his companion had arranged to meet him there.

Approaching his destination, turning over in his mind

some of the events which had taken place whilst the floating outfit had risked life and limb to clean up the town—it
having become notorious amongst trail crews from Texas
due to the unscrupulous activities of various citizens and
public officials—the blond giant was jolted from his reverie by the sounds of an altercation inside.

It was fortunate for Mark Counter that he was so large and
powerful!

There was a yell of mingled surprise and anger from
beyond the blond giant's range of vision. Then, hurtling
headlong through the batwing doors, came a big man
dressed after the fashion frequently adopted by celebrating
railroad construction workers. A smaller and lighter person
could hardly have avoided being knocked from the side-
walk by the impending collison, but Mark had the size and
heft to prevent such a fate befalling him. Thrusting his
hands forward, he halted and pushed aside the approaching
gandy dancer with no more discernible difficulty than if he
had been removing a toddling infant from his path. Having
done so, judging from the commotion that a fight was taking place, he strode into the bar-room of the Educated
Thirst Saloon to find out whether he would need to help
Erasmus O'Hagen's employees to bring it to an end.

With one exception, the sight which met the gaze of the
blond giant was pretty much as he had expected!

Whatever the cause might have been, the fighting had
already spread like ripples from a stone tossed into a pond
as the various occupants of the bar-room had become involved. Apart from the saloon's masculine workers, who
were trying to break up the brawl, the men present were
mainly cowhands and gandy dancers. However, a sprin-
kling of other Western occupations were represented, all of
whom had started to take sides either with the ranching or
railroad factions or against one another.

That Mark should see the other member of the floating outfit was actively engaged did not come as any surprise!

Tall, well made, in his mid-twenties, Red Blaze had pugnaciously good looking features and hair of such a fiery hue it explained how he had acquired his sobriquet. He dressed like the competent cowhand he could claim to be. However, such was his impetuous nature, he could always be counted upon to become a participant should there be fighting in his vicinity. Fortunately, he was a skilled performer in a roughhouse brawl such as was taking place.

Having taken one swift glance around, satisfied his companion needed no immediate help, the blond giant turned his full attention to the exception!

Almost equalling Mark in height and about the same age, albeit somewhat more bulky in build as he did not trim down nearly so well at the waist, the attire of the man in question suggested he too was a cowhand from Texas. However, to eyes which knew the West, there were indications that such might not necessarily be the case. The loss of his hat had brought into view soft brown hair grown longer than was considered acceptable by members of that fraternity. Furthermore, even as the blond giant was looking in that direction, a clutching hand wrenched off what was obviously a false beard. Doing so exposed a handsome face which, in spite of the prevailing conditions, bore an expression seemingly petulant rather than angry. Instead of having acquired the tan which normally resulted from working for long hours exposed to the elements, its skin texture was pallid. Furthermore, although there did not appear to be any reason for him to have donned such a thing, he had a black eye-patch fastened around his head and it was now pushed up on his brow.

Regardless of having features suggestive of a gentle, perhaps even pampered upbringing, the subject of Mark's attentions was proving himself a very competent barehanded fighter. Assailed from all sides by the gandy dancers, resembling—if such a thing was possible—a mild featured Texas flat-headed grizzly bear surrounded by a pack of big game hounds, he was using his big fists and feet with speed and to good effect. Nevertheless, unless he was to receive assistance, it seemed almost certain that he must eventually be worn down and defeated by sheer weight of numbers.

"*Cave adsum*, Cousin Mark!" the burly young man bellowed, on catching sight of the blond giant entering the bar-room. His voice was that of a well educated Southron as, without pausing in his extremely capable defense, he continued just as loudly, "How about coming to lend a deserving kinsman a hand?"

Having recognized his Cousin Trudeau even before hearing the motto of the Front de Boeuf family, "*Cave* adsum",[4] Mark wished their relationship had not been announced so publicly. Knowing the speaker, who was considered by practically all their relatives as being the "black sheep of the family," the blond giant suspected that the gandy dancers might have been given adequate cause for their hostile behaviour. His suppositions on that score were strengthened rather than diminished by having noticed the cowhand style clothing—their wearer having a disinclination to indulge in honest toil of any kind—and other suggestions that a disguise had been adopted. Nevertheless, like many Southrons in general and Texans in particular, he had been raised with a strong sense of responsibility to kinfolks. Therefore, snatching off his hat and sending it spinning through the air to fall behind the counter where he hoped it would be safe from

4. "*Cave adsum*," roughly translated from Latin, "Beware, I am here!" The researches of the world's foremost fictionist-genealogist, Philip Jose Farmer, *q.v.*, have established that Trudeau Front de Boeuf was a lineal descendant from Sir Reginald of the same name who was lord of Torquilstone Castle during the reign of King Richard the First of England, 1189-99: see; *Ivanhoe* by Sir Walter Scott. J.T.E.

damage, he was already advancing to render the requested aid.

On hearing what was shouted by Trudeau Front de Boeuf, three of the gandy dancers swung away from him and charged to intercept the blond giant. Being newly arrived from the East and having reached Trail End a short while before coming into the Educated Thirst Saloon, they did not realize against whom they would be in contention. Lacking this information and drawing an erroneous conclusion from his dandified appearance, they dismissed him as being nothing more dangerous than a dude who must be in cahoots with the man responsible for their animosity. On the other hand, taking into account his massive size, they also decided it might prove advisable to make a concerted attack rather than rushing at him individually.

Striding out faster in accordance with their companion's instructions, the men on the flanks converged towards Mark from either side. Waiting until they had started the final lunge for him, he stepped swiftly between them before their reaching hands could secure the holds they were seeking. As they were completely engrossed in their own intentions, the pair rushed into one another's arms on missing their target. Such was their eagerness to get to grips with the intruder, neither realized the mistake they were making and instinctively they started to grapple together. However, the big Texan was not allowed to capitalize upon this immediately.

Having produced a needed respite by contriving to divert some of his assailants against his cousin, who he was confident could handle them, Front de Boeuf started to make the most of the situation. Noticing an attacker was grabbing a chair by its seat and lifting it to be used as a club, he responded to threat with rapidity. Shooting out his left fist, covered by a black leather riding glove to prevent its white and uncalloused condition detracting from the rest of the disguise, he drove it straight through the bottom of the seat and into the face of the gandy dancer. Then, even as the recipient of the blow was going over backwards, Front de Boeuf sent a right footed kick into the stomach of another and was pounced upon from three sides by more of them.

Deftly blocking the punch directed at him by the third gandy dancer to come his way, the blond giant retaliated with a backhand swing to the side of the face. Despite the speed of its delivery, it sent the man in a racing twirl across the bar-room. Going over a table without it having reduced his speed, he rolled against a wall and lost all further interest in the proceedings. Utilizing the rest of the turning impetus employed while launching the blow, Mark swung around on his heel. Catching the other two would be attackers by the scruff of the neck, before they could separate from their entanglement, he rendered both of them *hors de combat* by banging their foreheads together.

On the point of continuing his attempt to render assistance to his cousin, whose shoulders were encircled from behind and his arms grasped on each side, the blond giant glanced at the mirror behind the bar. Its reflection of the scene warned him that the man who had been ejected was already coming back. Unfortunately, he made the discovery just a moment too late.

Having dashed over from the main entrance, the gandy dancer encircled and pinioned Mark's hands to his sides. As this happened a cavalry soldier, sent in their direction by a punch from Red Blaze, saw what he believed was an opportunity to repay the blow on another cowhand. Before he could do so, Mark brought up and thrust out both legs. The soles of the boots met the chest of the dark blue tunic and gave a shove which propelled its wearer in a hurried retreat. Although he managed to regain some control over his movements as he blundered backwards and turned, this proved less beneficial than he might have hoped. Having been returned towards his original assailant, he was given another blow to the jaw which sent him spinning into a corner. His head struck the wall and he limply collapsed.

Although the blond giant was prevented from reaching Front de Boeuf, who possessed enormous strength in his seemingly soft and well-padded body, he was able to escape unaided from the restraint being placed upon him. Having delivered a kick to the ribs which disposed of a gandy dancer coming to take advantage of his arms being held, he swung his torso from right to left and back. Such was the vigour he applied, the other three were unable to retain their grips and were pitched away from him. However, the man in the rear was less affected than his companions and was not thrown far. Snatching up a chair as he came to a halt, he returned to swing it against the back of the big Southron with all the force he could muster.

Supporting Mark's full weight during the removal of the soldier, the big gandy dancer could not help staggering under it or avoid loosening his rear bear hug hold a trifle. Bringing his feet to the floor again, the blond giant gave a spreading surge with his arms to separate these who had encircled him from behind. Having freed himself, with no more apparent difficulty than when he had halted the rush of the man outside, he pivoted swiftly around. The right cross to the chin he swung sent the gandy dancer from the bar-room at full speed. However, this time there was nobody to stop the man. The onlookers scattered as he emerged even faster than previously and at an angle which carried him to the hitching rail. Rolling over it, he alighted supine in the street and, after a feeble attempt to sit up, flopped flaccidly once more.

The attack made upon Front de Boeuf proved to be a mistake. Like all the furniture purchased by Erasmus O'Hagen for the bar-room, as a result of long experience in the saloon business, the chair was only made to stand up to normal use. Being employed as an improvised club, it shattered on impact. While this hurt the big Southron, it did not incapacitate him. It did, nevertheless, arouse his anger. All suggestion of petulance left his face. Its expression became such as his less than salubrious ancestor, Sir Reginald of Torquilstone Castle might have shown when aroused. Spinning around, he dealt his attacker a backhand right to the jaw which would in itself have been sufficient. Already rendered unconscious, the man was given a left to the solar plexus and a right swing to the other side of the jaw in rapid succession before his sagging body could move out of range. Sent sprawling, his no longer sentient body crashed into four fighters and knocked them from their feet.

"Red!" Mark bellowed, turning after he had sent the big gandy dancer flying from the bar-room. "Get over to Cousin Trudeau!"

Having considered the visit to Trail End far too tame to be enjoyable, the fiery haired cowhand had been delighted when the trouble started. Nor had he shown any hesitation in allowing himself to be drawn into the fray. However, as was his custom on joining the fighting, he had kept a tight rein upon his otherwise impetuous nature and had demonstrated a fistic ability of a high order. What was more, despite being actively engaged in the general brawling near the counter, he had seen Mark arrive and had heard what had been shouted.

"Yo!" Red replied, ducking beneath a punch and sending one of his own into the stomach of the thwarted deliverer.

Giving the traditional cavalry signification of assent and removing one obstacle by grabbing the shoulders and flinging aside the soldier he had hit, the red head set about doing as the blond giant had requested. Seeing his path would be blocked and probably disputed by some of the gandy dancers attacking Front de Boeuf, he ducked under table. Tilting it forward and grasping the lower p legs, he used it as a combined shield and batterin crash through and reach the big Southron. A moment later, knocking or throwing aside everybody who tried to stop him, the blond giant joined them.

"*Cave adsum*, Cousin Mark!" Front de Boeuf greeted. "Am I pleased to see you!"

"*Cave adsum!*" the blond giant replied, as he had when playing with the big Southron as children. "I thought you might be. Now let's get this whing-ding over, *pronto!*"

"Well now, boys," Town Marshal Stanley Woodrow Markham commented dryly, studying his surroundings as he entered the bar-room of the Educated Thirst Saloon followed by his deputies. His voice had an accent which suggested origins in Illinois and was surprisingly soft for a man of his size. "It looks like we would have been needed here, only we've come a mite too late."

The remark was justified!

Ably assisted by Red Blaze and Trudeau Front de Boeuf, Mark Counter had succeeded in doing as he had suggested when they had come together. Working as a team, they had first devoted their attention to quelling the gandy dancers. With this accomplished by their competent tactics, they had helped the staff of the saloon to deal with the other combatants. Felling everybody who had refused to cease hostilities when demanded verbally, they had quickly brought the rest of the fighting to an end. By the time the peace officers came on the scene, having been detained by other matters elsewhere in the town, all was peaceful and those customers who had surrendered were helping to bring around the unconscious men scattered about the room.

Thirty years of age, and somewhere between the blond giant and the big Southron in build, the marshal gave an impression of strength and power, backed by speed. Bare headed, his black hair was closely cropped. His ruggedly good looking features seemed enhanced rather than marred by the marks acquired during his successful career as a prize fighter. He had on a brown two-piece suit, a white shirt without a collar, and Hersome gaiter boots. Unlike his deputies, who wore gunbelts and carried sawed-off shotguns, he gave no sign of being armed. Nevertheless, his whole demeanour implied he was a man with whom it would not pay to trifle.

"All right, Alfred," Markham went on, feeling sure the trouble had not been provoked by members of the saloon's staff having tried to cheat some of the customers. "Start figuring out how much damage has got to be made good by these festive gents."

"Sure thing, Stan," assented Erasmus O'Hagen's floor manager who had the responsibility of running the saloon in the absence of his employer. He swung his gaze quickly over such of the tables, chairs and other fittings which had been broken during the fighting, assessing the cost of replacing them. Then he waved a hand towards the red head, the big Southron, and the blond giant, whose hat was being returned by a bartender. "It'd likely have come a heap higher happen Mark and these two fellers hadn't helped me and the boys to quieten the rest of them down."

"I'll keep that in mind," Markham promised and turned his attention to the trio. Having studied Red in a speculative and something close to an accusatory fashion for a moment, he continued, "What started the fussing, anyways?"

"I suppose it *could* be said that I did, marshal," Front de Boeuf confessed, as the two Texans and the floor manager looked in his direction.

"And just who might *you* be?" Markham inquired, taking in the pallid features and too long brown hair which struck him as being at odds with the speaker's attire of a cowhand.

"I'm Mark's cousin from New Orleans," the big Southron introduced, having heard enough whilst in Trail

End to realize his kinsman and the marshal were on good terms. Despite being disinclined to allow a peace officer to learn his true identity, he doubted whether the blond giant would render support for his explanation, which he felt sure was going to be required, should he attempt to supply an alias as he would otherwise have done. Therefore, reasonably certain he would not be known to Markham in such a fashion, he went on, "My name is Trudeau Front de Boeuf."

"Huh huh!" the marshal grunted non-committally, but nothing about him suggested he had ever before heard the name given by the big Southron. Nor did he so much as glance at Mark for confirmation of the announced relationship. Instead, keeping his gaze directed at Front de Boeuf, he continued, "So how did you come to start it?"

"Aw now, Stan, it wasn't his fault at all," Red protested. "It was those gandy dancers who caused all the fuss. They just couldn't take a friendly bit of joshing."

Good natured as well as impetuous, the fiery haired cowhand was ever willing to try to help anybody he regarded as a friend. Due to a sense of family loyalty having prevented Mark from mentioning the suspicions harboured by most of his kin where his Aunt Jessica and Cousin Trudeau were concerned, he had never spoken of them even to such close companions as the other members of the floating outfit.[5] Therefore, although they had not met previously, Red was willing to accept and offer his support to Front de Boeuf because of the relationship with his big blond *amigo*.

---

5. The reticence where the disreputable activities of Trudeau Front de Boeuf and his even more unscrupulous mother, Jessica, are concerned was continued until recently by the present day members of the Counter family. This led us to attribute an attempt to cause the death of Mark Counter to a "Cousin Cyrus" when producing the manuscript for: *Part Two, "We Hang Horse Thieves High," J.T.'S Hundredth*. However, we were allowed to clarify the situation in: *Cut One, They All Bleed*. J.T.E.

"Huh Huh!" Markham repeated, despite giving a nod as if wishing to indicate he would take into account the comment made by the cowhand. "Maybe *you'd* best tell me what happened, Mr. Front de Boeuf?"

"It was a joke which unfortunately wasn't appreciated and went wrong," the big Southron obliged. "You see, I only arrived this morning. I hadn't heard that Cousin Mark was in Trail End and, as I don't know anybody in town, I found myself at a bit of a loose end. So, as I was passing the saloon here, I thought I might be able to get acquainted with some of the customers if I came in and played a little trick which had helped me make friends in other places. In fact, I had had it in mind when I left the hotel and was carrying the glass eye and patch in my pocket——!"

"*Glass eye and patch?*" the marshal queried, the speaker having paused as though wishing to ensure his explanation was being followed. His tone became redolent of suspicion and his gaze went to where the latter item was still attached to the big man's forehead. "So you'd got them with you, huh?"

"I get the feeling you know the trick I mean," Front de Boeuf declared, without showing the slightest concern over the possibility. "Perhaps you read about it in the *Police Gazette* as I did?"

"I reckon I might have heard about it from somewheres," Markham answered and, although he believed he could guess, went on, "Tell me what you did, so's I'll know for sure whether I have or not."

"Of course, marshal," the Southron assented, exuding what appeared to be a genuine desire to please and a complete lack of any evil intent. "I put the patch over my right eye before I came in. At the bar, I claimed I had lost all my money playing poker and, pretending to take out the glass eye I was already holding, I offered to raffle it off at a dollar a time. It seemed that everybody was in good mood and entered into the spirit of the thing. Quite a few of them bought chances, so I borrowed one white chip and enough reds to cover the other entrants from the bartender, put them in my hat and let the draw be made. When the white chip came out, I told the man who had drawn it that I had a fiance who wouldn't marry me without my glass eye and offered to buy it back from him for five dollars. After he agreed and returned it, he asked me why I didn't put it back. Expecting to raise a laugh, as I always had in the past when pulling the trick, I lifted the patch to show my real eye and said, 'There wouldn't be any room for it, now would there?' "

"And that's when the fight started?" Markham stated rather than asked, the story having been pretty much as he had anticipated.

"As you say, that's when the fight started," Front de Boeuf confirmed, seeming contrite yet possessed of a clear conscience. "Instead of treating it as a joke and even before I could try to make amends by offering to buy drinks with the money I'd taken in the raffle, as I always do, those railroad workers became so abusive I was compelled to defend myself. I must say it would have gone very badly for me, outnumbered as I was, if Cousin Mark hadn't happened by so fortuitously."

"That's just how it happened, Stan," Red asserted, without waiting to be asked for confirmation. "When all those gandy dancers jumped him, I reckoned the odds were too far out of line and figured I'd help to even them a mite. Which's how come everybody else took cards."

"Knowing *you* from back when, I figured it was something of the kind," the marshal claimed, but in an amiable fashion. However, his tone became neutral once more as he returned his attention to the big Southron. "You don't strike me as being a working cowhand, Mr. Front de Boeuf. So how come you're dressed like one?"

"For convenience," the Southron replied. "As you guessed, I'm *not* a working cowhand. In fact, I'm one of those fortunate beings whose family is sufficiently wealthy for me to have no need to do work of any kind. However, as I know Westerners tend to indulge in horse-play when meeting a dude, I've found dressing like a cowhand saves me from being subjected to such treatment."

Watching and listening to Front de Boeuf, Markham had mixed emotions. His suspicions, already aroused by concluding the Southron was not a working cowhand, had been increased when the glass eye and patch were mentioned. However, he had received a feasible explanation as to how the knowledge of the use to which they could be put had been acquired. Although he had not seen the issue, he was aware that the *Police Gazette* frequently had articles describing how confidence tricks were carried out. Furthermore, the selection of the clothing had been explained by a reason which was justified. Nevertheless, despite the Southron also being related to a man in whose honesty he had complete trust, the marshal felt distinctly uneasy without being able to decide why this should be.

For his part, the blond giant was plagued by equally disturbed emotions. Knowing his cousin justified the misgivings held by many of their relations, his law abiding nature was at odds with his ingrained sense of loyalty to kinfolks. He had a suspicion that, even if the raffling of the glass eye was intended just to get acquainted with the other occupants of the saloon, there had been an ulterior motive.

"Mind if I suggest something, Stan?" Mark requested, seeing a way by which he could achieve a compromise between his conscience and family loyalty.

"Go to it," Markham authorized.

"Nobody's been hurt worse than a few bumps, lumps and bruises in the fighting," the blond giant pointed out, waving his right hand to indicate the various participants who were regaining consciousness. "So, happen Cousin Trudeau pays half of the damages himself, being well able to afford it, why don't we forget what's happened and all go on our way friendly?"

"The boss'd go for that," supported the floor manager.

"Well, Mr. Front de Boeuf," the marshal said, considering the suggestion was more than fair, and was likely to appeal even to the gandy dancers when they were told of it. Like any decent peace officer, particularly when dealing with the various factions which came to a Kansas Railroad and trail end town, he was eager to avoid friction between them while ensuring justice was done. "How do you feel about it?"

For a moment, the big Southron did not reply!

As Mark had suspected, Front de Boeuf had used the raffling of the glass eye as a way of establishing himself in a favourable fashion with the other customers. It had been his intention to use the money for the purchase of drinks. Then he had had every expectation of reaping a handsome profit from the poker game he was planning to start. Unfortunately, having failed to take into account that a gandy dancer might resent being made the butt of a joke by someone who appeared to be a cowboy, the fight had spoiled his plans.

Glancing at his cousin, the Southron read a warning that he must accept the terms or forfeit any further support. He also felt the surge of admiration which always arose when they were together. Although he stood to gain a considerable fortune should Mark die in certain circumstances, he had never lost his liking for his kinsman. As children, the blond giant alone was stronger than him and yet had never presumed upon his superiority. Furthermore, Mark was one of the few members of the family who had never called him by the hated sobriquet, "Cyrus," which derived from the name of his father who had been deserted by his mother while he was still a baby.

"Very well, marshal," Front de Boeuf replied, yielding to the inevitable and having sufficient money available to make the payment without being left in dire straits. "Tell me what my share will be and I'll pay for it now."

"Get your hands up, Barrington-Bygrave, or whatever god-damned summer name you're using!" commanded a harsh, mid-Western voice before any more could be said.

Noticing the words had a disturbing effect upon his cousin, Mark Counter joined the other men in his group as they looked towards the speaker!

Standing just inside the batwing doors of the bar-room, holding a sawed-off shotgun in a position of readiness, was a sharp and sallow featured man of middle age and medium size. From the black Derby hat perched at the back of his balding head, through a loud pinstriped three piece suit, salmon pink shirt and gaudy multi-hued cravat, to his blunt-toed black boots, he had the appearance of being a city dweller. For all that, he had on a Western style gunbelt with a Colt Civilian Model Peacemaker revolver in the cross draw holster at the left side. Furthermore, attached to his vest and displayed prominently, the badge of a United States' deputy marshal indicated why he was not conforming with the civic ordinance which banned the bearing of firearms in Trail End.

"Don't you try nothing smart assed, big feller!" the newcomer warned as he walked forward. His whole attention and the twin barrels of the shotgun were directed towards Trudeau Front de Boeuf. "You're not toting that fancy whipit gun's you're so slick at using and this scatter of mine'll copper any other bet you're figuring on pulling and'll holler 'keno' to it."

"The way you're talking, deputy," Markham commented, having darted a quick glance at Mark and received a blank stare in return, "Seems like you reckon you know this gent." He was aware that the kind of weapon to which the man he was addressing had referred was a shotgun with the barrels and butt cut down for concealment purposes, until it was not much longer than a Colt Cavalry Model Peacemaker.

"It's a whole slew more'n just plain '*reckon*,' marshal," the man with the shotgun and badge corrected with assurance. "He's wanted down to Dodge City and in other places, likely, for pulling confidence games."

"I'm afraid, *officer*, that you have got the *wrong* man," Trudeau Front de Boeuf denied in a polite tone, but he stood as if turned to stone.

"Like hell I have," the newcomer countered. "Just last week, you and your momma took down Senator Anthony Billinghurst with the old 'Proof of Trust' game in Dodge.[6] Which I don't reckon's how he's the first, nor the only one, you pair've flim-flammed."

"I've not the slightest idea of what this *gentleman* is talking about, marshal!" the big Southron claimed, with what appeared to be righteous indignation. "While I remember having read about the trick to which he referred in the *Police Gazette*, I assure you I've never even thought of trying it. As I said, *officer*, I can only assume you are mistaking me for someone else."

"The only god-damned mistake that's been made is you letting me see you in here," the man with the shotgun stated, the final sentence having been directed to him. "Stick your hands out so's the marshal can 'cuff 'em for me!"

"Now just hold hard there for a minute!" Markham put

---

6. A description of how the "Proof of Trust" confidence trick is carried out can be found in: *Part Three, "Birds Of A Feather," Wanted! Belle Starr.* J.T.E.

in, studying Front de Boeuf speculatively. The suspicions aroused earlier had been stirred again by Mark remaining silent instead of speaking in defense of the big Southron, but he was too experienced to be rushed into something which might prove wrong. "Before I start putting handcuffs on *anybody*, I'd sooner know's they belong there. Do you have a warrant for this gent, deputy, or anything else's will *prove* he's who you say he is?"

"Well, no," the newcomer admitted sullenly. Then, transferring his left hand from the foregrip of the shotgun to the inside pocket of his jacket and bringing something out, he went on, "Maybe I can't come straight out and say's how I do, but there's something in here's'll prove I'm U.S. Deputy Marshal Elmer Quincy."

"Huh huh!" Markham grunted, finding the noncommittal utterance as useful as he had in the past. Accepting the wallet he was offered, he compared the of necessity brief description on the official identification card with the appearance of the man who had handed it over and decided they matched. "I'm satisfied that you're who you say you are. Thing being, are you *certain* this's the feller you're after?"

"He's not dressed anywhere near's fancy as usual, I'll admit," Quincy replied, taking back and returning the wallet to the inside pocket. "But I'd recognize that momma's boy face of his anywheres and could pick him out no matter what he's wearing, nor how big the crowd. So, happen you'll put the 'cuffs on him for me, I'll have him on the next train back to Dodge."

"Not so fast," the marshal requested politely, remembering that he had never heard of anybody related to Mark Counter being involved in criminal activities. "Can you show us something that will prove the deputy's making a mistake about you, Mr. Front de Boeuf?"

"Well no, I'm afraid I can't," the big Southron answered, somehow contriving to sound as if he considered the omission was a reflection upon the two peace officers rather than himself. "Unfortunately, as I wasn't intending to make an extended stay in your city and couldn't possibly have envisaged the necessity might arise, I didn't trouble to carry any papers with me. However, perhaps it will satisfy you if Cousin Mark will vouch for me?"

"I've never seen Cousin Trudeau do anything dishonest," the blond giant declared, which was true as far as it went and served as a compromise between his conscience and family loyalty, in response to the interrogative glance turned his way by Markham.

"Which don't prove's how he ain't done nothing when you wasn't looking," Quincy pointed out, before the local peace officer could speak. "I'm giving you my word as a U.S. deputy marshal's I know he's the conjuneero who took down Senator Billinghurst. So I'm doing my sworn and bounden duty by arresting him and taking him with me."

"There's no train before noon tomorrow," Markham answered. "And, while I'm not saying if you're acting right, seeing's how it'll come back to me as well as you if you should be, I want to see a warrant and some other papers describing him before you take him out of my bailiwick. Tell you what we'll do. You telegraph your boss to send them along by the westbound train, so's they'll be here in the morning. 'Tween times, I'll hold him down to the jailhouse and, once I've seen them, I'll not only let you take him, I'll have a couple of my deputies go along if you're so minded."

"Why Aunt Jessica, this is a *surprise*!" Mark Counter ejaculated, opening the door of his hotel room in response to a knock. "Cousin Trudeau didn't say anything about you coming to Trail End!"

"He didn't know I was," replied the woman in the passage, walking across the threshold without waiting to be invited. Her demeanour and carriage were indicative of arrogance, but her rich contralto Southern accent had no discernible emotion as she went on, "Have you heard what happened?"

"The marshal told me," the blond giant answered and nodded to the other male occupant of the room. "That's why Red and I are still here."

Realizing Markham was adamant upon the handling of the situation, Quincy had signified a grudging acquiescence. Having no illusions where his cousin was concerned, even though he would not have made such an admission publicly, Mark had believed the accusation could be justified. Therefore, he had made no attempt to intercede in behalf of Front de Boeuf. In fact, appreciating that Markham was giving his cousin the benefit of the doubt on account of their relationship, he had been ready to use his own influence if necessary. The need had not arisen. Warning how serious the consequences of wrongful arrest could be, clearly directing the words at Quincy and not the local peace officer, the big Southron had raised no objections to being dealt with as the latter had stipulated.

Taken to the jailhouse and placed in a cell, with the Texans allowed to accompany him, Front de Boeuf had handed over sufficient money to cover his share in the payment for the damage caused during the fighting at the Educated Thirst Saloon. Learning that his mother was not in Trail End, Markham had asked whether he wanted her to be informed by telegraph of his plight. He had declined on the grounds that, particularly as he was confident the matter could easily be straightened out when he was returned to Dodge City, he did not want to cause her needless distress. Wondering whether his cousin was innocent and a victim of mistaken identity, or perhaps had aroused the animosity of the United States' deputy marshal in some way and was being victimized by this, Mark had inquired whether there was anything he could do. Saying both could wait until morning, the big Southron had requested that his belongings be collected from the room he was occupying at the best hotel in town and the bill paid. Promising to attend to this and have a meal sent in, the blond giant had gone about his business.

Having told Red Blaze something about his cousin, the blond giant had stated they would both put the matter from their minds. Satisfied that his big *amigo* knew best, the fiery haired cowhand had done as he was told and they had spent an enjoyable evening as they had planned.

While the Texans were eating breakfast in the dining-room of the slightly less expensive hotel in which they were accommodated, prior to doing as had been promised to Front de Boeuf, Markham had arrived. He had told them that, just before midnight, Quincy had visited the jailhouse with two companions. When the solitary deputy acting as turnkey had refused to release the Southron into their custody without written authority from his superior, they had clubbed him insensible. Then they had opened the cell and taken Front de Boeuf with them. According to the only other prisoner, who had been left bound and gagged as had the turnkey, the Southron had not gone willingly. In fact, the trio had tied his hands and arms securely as a means of compelling him to accompany them. Because the town was in a peaceful condition all night, there had been no reason for the marshal or any of his other deputies to visit the office. Therefore, the incident had not been discovered until the first of them had reported for duty that morning.

Knowing Mark would be interested, after having ascertained that he could not suggest any reason why his cousin should have been incarcerated at the instigation of the obviously bogus U.S. deputy marshal and then abducted, Markham had described the action taken so far. It was not much. A telegraph message had been sent to the United States' marshal in the State capitol, warning him that a man was masquerading as a member of his department. As yet, however, no posse had been organized to go in pursuit of Quincy's party. The prisoner had not heard anything of them after they had left the jailhouse, so it was impossible to determine in which direction they had gone.

Promising to keep the Texans informed of all developments, especially if his deputies—who were going around town asking questions—should learn anything to help him decide where he should start searching, the marshal had left to attend to his duties. Mark and Red had carried out the instructions given by Front de Boeuf, bringing his belongings to the former's room. Having done so, they had settled down to await developments. Hearing the knock on the door, they had expected it was somebody sent by Markham with news that the requisite information had been received.

Coming to his feet from where he had been relaxing on the bed, Red studied the woman as she swept, rather than entered into the room. He could see nothing to suggest that she was feeling distress, needless or otherwise, although she was obviously aware of what had happened. On the other hand, it was plain to him from where the massive physique of the big Southron had been inherited.

In any company, Jessica Front de Boeuf would have been an imposing figure.[7] Five foot nine in height, her Junoesque body still retained the curvaceous fullness of its "hourglass" contours despite having led a life in which lit-

---

7. When not using an alias in some illegal scheme, seeking to annoy and embarrass her family for having cast her out, Jessica Front de Boeuf employed her maiden name and not that of the husband she had deserted soon after their marriage. J.T.E.

tle restraint had been exercised where the "pleasures of the flesh" were concerned. She had on a Wavelean hat secured by a decorative pin to elegantly piled up black hair which made her appear even taller. Although the texture of the skin was beginning to coarsen a trifle more than could be hidden by make-up, her olive skinned face was beautiful if marred somewhat by lines indicative of an arrogant and domineering nature. Stylish and revealing to the point of being close to *risque*, her navy blue two-piece travelling costume and lime-green blouse were obviously expensive. The jewellery which glistened about her neck, from the lobes of her ears, on her wrists and hands appeared to be equally costly. She carried a gaily coloured parasol in her right hand and a reticule dangled by its strap from her left.

"The town marshal told me you were here, nephew," the beautiful newcomer announced, after having given Red a glance redolent of disapproval. "But I hoped I would find you alone."

"I'll go and wait in my room, *amigo*," the fiery haired cowhand offered, starting to walk away.

"There's no call for that," the blond giant asserted. "Stay put!"

"Really, nephew, this is a *family* matter!" Jessica objected, her manner frigid, directing a glare to where Red had come to a halt. "I hardly think it proper for us to speak in front of a *stranger*!"

"Red's no stranger to *me*," Mark stated, firmly yet politely. He decided his aunt was as imperious as he always remembered her to be. "Allow me to present Charles Henry Blaze. His uncle is General Ole Devil Hardin and you can count on his discretion like my own."

"But——!" the woman began.

"Tru's in bad trouble, 'less I miss my guess, Aunt Jessica!" the blond giant interrupted. "And, happen I'm going to help get him out of it, I'm going to need some backing I can count on from here to there and back the long ways. Which Red's a real good man to be giving it."

"Very well!" the woman assented, but with the bad grace of one who only rarely had her wishes thwarted: "Have it *your* way!"

"I reckon we can talk this out a whole heap easier was we to do it sitting down," Mark suggested. Waiting until his aunt had taken the chair by the dressing-table which he had indicated, while he and the other Texan occupied opposite ends of the bed facing her, he continued, "First thing is, did you and Cousin Tru pull the 'Proof of Trust' game on Senator Billinghurst in Dodge?"

"*Really*, nephew!" Jessica snorted, exuding what appeared to be genuine indignation. "How could you thin——?"

"Did you?" the blond giant insisted, giving no indication of being convinced by the response he had elicited.

"We most certainly did *not*!" the woman declared, just as vehemently, but decided against pretending ignorance of the "Proof of Trust" confidence trick. "Whatever made you think we did?"

"That was the reason the *hombre* reckoning to be a deputy U.S. marshal gave for having Cousin Tru tossed into the pokey," Mark explained, feeling sure his aunt would not chance lying about something which could be checked without difficulty by sending a telegraph message to the authorities in Dodge City. "Knowing Tru like I do, I don't need to ask why the feller wanted him jailed. He'd be a whole heap safer to take while he was in a cell than while he was roaming around loose and with room to fight. So the thing being, what did Quincy want with him?"

"*Want* with him?" Jessica queried, looking as if baffled by the question.

"Want with him," the blond giant reiterated. "We know now that Quincy wasn't a peace officer doing his duty, or maybe hoping to collect a reward from the Senator he reckoned you'd wronged. And he had to have a real good reason for taking the chance of pretending to be a deputy U.S. marshal so's he could have Cousin Tru handcuffed for him by the marshal, or tossed in the pokey when that didn't pan out, and then busting him loose. So why did he go to all that trouble?"

"For *money*, of course!" the woman claimed, with the air of stating the obvious and considering nothing more could be said. Nevertheless, reaching into her reticule, she produced and opened a sheet of paper. "This was waiting for me when I got to the hotel and asked for my room."

"What is it?"

"A ransom note demanding that I pay eight thousand dollars for his return."

"Do you have that kind of money?" Mark asked, taking and reading the message written in a sprawling hand.

"I don't," Jessica replied, then paused and her voice took on a different tone as she continued, "Not yet anyw—— They must have been fooled by the high-toned name we're using and the way we dress and live, so thought I'm wealthy enough to be able to afford that much money."

"Come on now, Aunt Jessica!" Mark growled, although the suggestion after her second pause had been made with what many people would have believed to be a sincere conviction and in a different timbre to the words which preceded it. "I want the *truth*!"

"*Really*, nephew!" the woman gasped, her attitude seeming to insinuate that she resented her word being doubted. "Are you implying that I'm a li——?"

"The marshal *might* have believed those jaspers just thought you're rich, happen you told him about the ransom," the blond giant put in coldly. "He doesn't *know* you. But you're talking to *me* now and I do. So I want the truth, or we're pulling up stakes right now. Should we do it, no matter whether you convinced Stan Markham or not, he's smart enough to start wondering why we've gone instead of sticking around to give you any help we can."

"Do you mean to tell me that you'd *desert* a member of your own *family* at such a time?" Jessica demanded. "I expected *better* of you, Mark Counter."

"It'll be all your own doing if we go," the blond giant pointed out, showing no contrition. "Family responsibility or not, there's something going on you don't want us to know about. For one thing, Quincy didn't think you're just rich folks. What he said, he knew you bend the law a mite on occasion———!"

"*Really*, nephew———!" Jessica yelped. "How dare you say such a thing in front of———!"

"So I don't aim to have Red and me sitting in on something that could wind up with us having to lock horns with the law," Mark continued, as if the interruption had not taken place. "Which being, either you tell us what it's really about, or we're lighting a shuck for Mulrooney this afternoon!"

Despite having decided that her nephew had every intention of carrying out the ultimatum, Jessica Front de Boeuf did not speak for almost thirty seconds!

Hoping to elicit support from the other occupant of the room, who she believed might prove susceptible to the kind of manipulation at which she was most adept, the beautiful woman turned a look of well simulated pleading in his direction which she had found worked on other occasions.

Studying Red Blaze with the calculation of one who had derived much of her far from frugal livelihood from exploiting masculine weaknesses, Jessica was disappointed by what she read in the freckled and pugnaciously good looking features. There was no suggestion of her having aroused the sympathy she required. In fact, the way she was having her gaze returned warned her that she must revise the impression she had had of him so far.

At first sight, the woman had dismissed the fiery haired cowhand as merely having been brought to Trail End by her nephew to provide companionship. Her revised judgement warned he was much more than that. Reckless and impetuous as he might prove in some circumstances, she felt sure he would also become competent and capable enough when the need arose. Therefore, if she could win him over, he would be as useful an ally as the blond giant; albeit one more pliable to her will. She also concluded that, no matter what she might have been able to accomplish had they been alone, he would follow the lead of her nephew in the prevailing conditions.

"Very well!" Jessica yielded sullenly, accepting she would have to show a certain amount of frankness if she wanted to obtain the assistance which she knew she would require if her theory on the kidnapping was correct. "I can't bring anybody called 'Quincy' to mind. What does he look like?"

"Does he come to mind now?" Mark asked, after describing the man who had posed as a United States' deputy marshal.

"No, I can't say he does," the woman admitted, having thought for a few seconds. "At least, as far as I know, he isn't one of Kent Bruce's regular men."

"And who-all's this 'Kent Bruce' *hombre*?" the blond giant asked.

"A *business* associate," the woman supplied, placing great emphasis upon the second word. "We're engaged in some most *private* and very *confidential* negotiations which I'm not at liberty to discuss further, even with *you*, nephew. All I can say is, I have something he wants and is willing to pay a high price to get."

"Would this price run's high as eight thousand dollars, ma'am?" Red suggested, before his *amigo* could continue the questioning.

"Slightly higher," Jessica understated, the deal calling for a payment of ten thousand dollars, deciding the comment indicated the fiery haired cowhand was thinking along similar lines to her own and was proving her summation with regards to his intelligence.

"I won't ask what this Kent Bruce *hombre* wants from you and don't want telling," Mark stated firmly, wanting one matter settled before they went any further in the discussion. Having no doubt the "private and very confidential negotiations" were illegal, he was still striving to keep the balance between his conscience and responsibility to kinfolks. "But will whatever it is happen here in Trail End?"

"It won't," the woman assured and, watching her carefully, the blond giant decided she was speaking the truth.

"Just so it *isn't*," Mark drawled, but his aunt read a note of warning in his voice. "Now I get the notion that you're like Red and me. You reckon this Bruce *hombre*'s behind Cousin Tru being grabbed off by Quincy."

"I *may* be doing him an injustice," Jessica declared. "But it is a possibility."

"Then how come Cousin Tru was here alone?" the blond giant wanted to know. "I'd've thought that, with something like whatever it is you're got going, you'd've stuck together."

"Normally we would have, particularly with Edward being laid up by a bullet wound," Jessica admitted, referring to a man who travelled with her and did her bidding. "In fact, the arrangement was for us to get together with Mr. Bruce here yesterday. Then something came up which detained me in Dodge City, so I sent Trudeau to meet and tell him I would follow with the—to conclude our negotiations—today."

"Who-all picked Trail End for the meeting, ma'am?" Red put in.

"Mr. Bruce," the woman replied.

"Then this can't be his home range?" Red asked, although the words were more in the style of a statement.

"He doesn't even live near here," Jessica confirmed. "Why?"

"I didn't reckon you'd be willing to dicker with him on his own stomping grounds," the red head replied. "And those three jaspers who wide-looped your boy couldn't've been local-grown, else the deputy they whomped'd've recognized them before there'd be chance to do it."

"So?" the woman prompted, the summation being much like her own.

"So'd they have to have some local help," Red elaborated. "Somebody who knows the range hereabouts and could pick a place where they could hide up with your boy until you pay the ransom."

"That's true," Jessica confirmed.

"Would this Bruce *hombre* know anybody to do it?" Red inquired.

"He's sure to have a contact locally, he does in most places," the woman replied. "But I've no idea who it might be."

"That's a pity, ma'am," the red head claimed. "If you had, it could either've helped us figure out where-at they're hiding out with your boy. Or we could've maybe grabbed the jasper and made him tell us."

"But we *don't* know!" Jessica pointed out, forcing herself to restrain the impatience of her imperious nature.

"No, ma'am, we don't," Red conceded, looking from the blond giant to the wardrobe in which they had placed Trudeau Front de Boeuf's belongings on collection from the other hotel. "And, happen we're lucky, Bruce doesn't know yet whether they've got your boy or not."

"I don't follow you!" the woman stated, finding it more difficult to control her irascibility.

"Well now, ma'am," the red head replied. "Happen Bruce doesn't know if they've got Tru yet, he's likely going to want to know the why-not of it should he be taken with the notion that they *haven't* got him."

"Howdy there, Mr. Bruce," Michael Murdock greeted, in his whining Mid-West accent. His tall and raw boned figure and cheap attire suggesting he was a not over affluent farmer. Although he owned a small place some five miles west of Trail End, he did little work on it and did not rely upon its produce for his livelihood. His manner was deferential as he looked at the shorter of the two passengers he had come to meet from the east-bound train. "Quincy and his boys've grabbed off that big feller like you told 'em to——!"

"If they said I knew anything about it, they're liars!" interrupted the man to whom the words were addressed. "And don't you forget it!"

Of medium height, plump to the point of obesity, Kent Bruce wore clothing of the latest Eastern style which were expensive and in excellent taste. His features seemed bland and generally gave the impression of amiability, only rarely offering even a hint of his true, completely unscrupulous nature. Those who knew him well were aware that, beyond the apparent mild joviality was a core of ruthless and cold bloodedly efficient evil.

Being pernicious at heart, Bruce had been disinclined to meet the high price demanded by Jessica Front de Boeuf for certain vital information regarding a very large shipment of gold which she had acquired on his behalf. However, knowing she could easily dispose of it elsewhere and would not hesitate to do so regardless of having been commissioned by him to procure it, he had concocted a scheme intended to reclaim the majority of the money. Having arranged to meet her on what amounted to neutral ground, he had been too wise to use any of the men who could be connected with him. Approached with the plan, Quincy had insisted upon being paid a deposit and having the rest of the balance on Bruce's arrival at Trail End. As the bogus United States' deputy marshal had not been shown the ransom note left for the woman by Murdock and was unaware that he would be receiving five thousand dollars less than demanded, the stipulation had been accepted. Nevertheless, Bruce had no intention of admitting his complicity to one he regarded as an underling.

"I won't forget it, boss!" Murdock promised. "Only they said's how you'd have the rest of their money for 'em 'n' I was to fetch it along so's they can get going."

"What's their rush?" Bruce demanded.

"They said's how they wanted to make sure of having a good head start afore his momma pays to get him turned loose," the go-between replied.

"Or maybe them—and *you*—figure the boss for a sucker?"

Hearing the comment, made in a harsh voice which was Northern in origin, Murdock swung a worried gaze at the speaker. Close to six foot in height, middle-aged, lean, with leathery and heavily moustached features, his attire was that of the Montana range country. The gunbelt he had on carried two Colt Civilian Model Peacemakers in its fast draw holsters and, to Western eyes, he was likely to prove competent in their use. Knowing this to be a fact where David Yorath was concerned, the go-between felt decidedly uneasy.

"How do you mean, Dave?" Bruce demanded.

"Look across there!" Yorath requested, gesturing across the street with the pigskin valise belonging to his employer which he was carrying as well as his own carpetbag.

Bruce and Murdock followed his gesture and reacted in a way which was different and yet in some ways similar!

The former let out a hiss of angry surprise and the latter gasped in amazement as they saw two figures looking their way from just inside the mouth of an alley further along and at the other side of the street. Apparently wanting to be detected and approached, the beautiful black haired woman and her massive, also well dressed, companion withdrew quickly behind the nearer building.

"What's the game, damn you?" Bruce challenged, when the couple did not appear again, swinging a face which was no longer either bland or amiable to glare at the lanky man. "That was Jessica Coeur de Lion and her son across there."

"That wasn't what Quincy called him, boss!" Murdock croaked, being more alarmed by the change which had come over the master criminal than from noticing Yorath was putting down the bags to leave both hands free. "But we've got him out at my place!"

"How can you have him out at your place?" the hard-case demanded, mocking the way in which the go-between had made the statement. "Or, *if* you have, who in hell was that over in the alley with her?"

"I—I dunno," Murdock admitted worriedly, then had an inspiration. "Maybe it's just some young feller she's got to keep herself all bedded down and happy?"

"And maybe the moon's made of green cheese!" Bruce snorted. "While I'll not deny dear Jessica's more than a mite hot-assed, there aren't all that many young men around with the size and heft of her son."

"So what's the god-damned game, plough-pusher?" Yorath supplemented.

"I—I tell you they fetched the feller they reckoned was the one the boss wan—they'd been told to get out to my place," Murdock insisted. "Unless——!"

"Unless *what*?" Bruce wanted to know.

"Unless they got the wrong feller," the go-between of-fered. "Come to think of it, even though his face was too pale for working out of doors and his hands real soft 'n' white, he was wearing cowhand duds." Noticing a man coming towards them, he went on, "Watch out, boss. It's the new town clown!"

"Howdy, gents," Stan Markham greeted, strolling up. However, his gaze was directed at the hard-case alone as he continued, "I reckon you saw the signs on the walls of the depot?"

"*Signs*?" Yorath repeated, despite knowing what was implied by the question. "What *signs* would they be?"

"The big ones with bright red ink, saying the wearing of guns within the city limits is banned by civic ordinance," the marshal explained, with what appeared to be mild politeness. "Which being, I'll take your gunbelt now and you can pick it up from the jailhouse just before you leave town."

"Like he——!" the hard-case began truculently, having noticed the peace officer was not wearing arms in view.

"Do as the marshal asks, Mr. Yorath!" Bruce commanded, knowing his bodyguard had a quick temper and, particularly in the prevailing conditions, wanting to avoid trouble. "The law is the law and it behooves us, as honest citizens, to uphold it."

"Whatever you say, boss!" the hard-case assented sullenly.

"Thanks, *mister*!" Markham said, accepting the belt and weapons offered to him with more than a suggestion of reluctance. "Enjoy your stay in Trail End, gents, but keep in mind the ordinance means no guns of any kind, whether worn openly or concealed, can be toted around town."

"We'll keep it in mind, marshal," Bruce promised, although the words had been intended for his bodyguard as they all knew. "But what if my colleague needs to go out of town on business?"

"He can come by the office and pick up his guns when

he's ready to leave," Markham replied. "But I'll want them handed in again as soon as he gets back."

"That's fair enough," Bruce claimed, seemingly filled with bonhomie and good will. "And a most sensible ruling, if I may say so."

"We like it," the marshal declared, dangling the gunbelt over his broad left shoulder. "Enjoy your stay."

"God damned, small town tin-star son-of-a-bitch!" Yorath snarled, glowering after the departing peace officer.

"I suppose he might be," Bruce replied dryly. "But you getting into trouble with him won't serve *my* purpose. So, as long as you're being well paid by me, I'll thank you to keep that in mind."

"Sure, boss," the hard-case assented, being too wise to cross his employer. "Why'd you ask about me leaving town?"

"Because that's what you're going to do," Bruce explained.

"But you said you wanted me with you while you was dickering with her," Yorath objected, knowing his employer had arranged to have him present.

"I do, so I'll make sure I keep out of her way until you're back," Bruce answered. "Get a horse for Mr. Yorath, Murdock. Then take him out to your place so he can find out what's going on."

Sharing a two-bedroom suite with his employer at the second best hotel in Trail End, knowing "Jessica Coeur de Lion" would be at the superior establishment, David Yorath was on his way downstairs to carry out his orders.

Like any man who earned a living as a hired gun fighter, the hard-case was never at ease when having to appear in public without his weapon belt and revolvers strapped on. Therefore, despite intending to go straight to the jailhouse and retrieve them, he could not resist the temptation to arm himself while waiting for Michael Murdock to arrive with the horses. Removing the short barrelled Colt Storekeeper Model Peacemaker carried in his carpetbag for such contingencies, he tucked it into the waistband of his trousers behind his back so it was concealed beneath his calfskin vest. With this done, he had kept watch from the window until seeing the go-between was approaching on a horse and leading another clearly rented from a not too expensive livery stable.

Realizing he was faced with a fairly long ride upon such a poor mount, Yorath was in a far from amiable mood as he descended from his room on the second floor. Apart from instinctively noticing they were all obeying the civic ordinance banning the wearing of firearms, he paid no attention to a group of Texans standing engaged in cheerful conversation in the centre of the reception lobby. However, as he was passing, one of them turned and, by accident it seemed, not only bumped into him but stepped heavily upon his right toes. Intended as an aid to digging into the ground for added security when roping on foot, the high heel of the boot inflicted pain which did nothing to improve the hard-case's already far from good temper.

"Hey, I'm sorry, mis——!" the cowhand began.

"God damn you for a clumsy beef-hand son-of-a-bitch!" Yorath spat out, glaring into an apologetic freckled, good looking face between fiery red hair and a tightly rolled silk bandana which was a riot of violently contrasting colours.[8]

"I said I was sorry, mister!" Red Blaze pointed out, with a mildness which might have surprised anybody who knew him. "There's no call for you to go mean-mouthing me that way!"

---

8. How Charles Henry "Red" Blaze came into possession of the distinctive multi-coloured silk bandana is told in: *Part Two, "Cousin Red's Big Chance," The Hard Riders.* J.T.E.

"I'll do more than just mean-mouth you if you don't get the hell away from me!" Yorath threatened, starting to walk onwards.

"Aw come on now, mister," Red said, adopting a placatory tone and catching the hard-case by the left bicep. "Let me buy you a drink to make up f——!"

"Get away from me!" Yorath commanded furiously, snatching free his arm and spinning on his heel to launch a punch with it.

Alert for such a possibility, although it was not entirely the response he was hoping to produce, the red haired Texan ducked beneath the blow. Coming up after having avoided it, he retaliated with a backhand slap from his right knuckles. Caught on the cheek as painfully as his toes had suffered, the hard-case was driven back a step. Then, despite having tried to use his fist, he elected to return to the means he usually adopted when his temper was aroused. Spluttering a profanity, he sent his right hand behind his back to close around the butt of the concealed revolver.

Gliding swiftly forward as he saw what Yorath was doing, Red started to counter the threat. His left hand caught and gave the hard-case's bent right elbow an outwards and upwards thrust. Nor did he rely upon this alone to save him. Although his action had put Yorath in an awkward position, he knew he was still not out of danger. Therefore, he passed his right hand between the one he had struck and the hard-case's body. Working in smooth co-ordination, he contrived to grasp the wrist with both his hands. He was too late to prevent the weapon being freed from the waistband, so gave a quick snapping motion to jerk it downwards and back. Continuing the rearwards movement, which locked the hard-case's elbow and wrist, he ensured the barrel was at no time pointed in his direction.

Competently as the red head was acting, it seemed he

was not going to have everything his own way!

Caught unawares by the speed and efficiency with which he was being tackled, Yorath recovered sufficient of his presence of mind to resist. His torso was inclined forward by the twisted right arm being raised, but he was still contriving to retain his hold on his revolver. What was more, he sent a kick with his right foot which reached the inside of his captor's left leg. As it landed, he felt the grip upon his trapped wrist loosen a trifle. Not enough for him to jerk it free, but he was able to twist and slam his left fist into the Texan's ribs. Despite the awkward position from which it was thrown, the blow caused him to be released.

Having escaped, a realization of how close he had come to the humiliation of being disarmed in public filled the hard-case with an uncontrollable rage. Moving away from his surprisingly capable assailant, he was determined to take revenge. Without a single thought for the possible consequences if he succeeded, he straightened up and started to bring his Colt towards where the unarmed Texan was preparing to resume the attack.

Before the weapon could be turned into alignment upon Red, Stan Markham appeared in the front entrance. Giving a bellowed command for the gun to be dropped, he hurtled forward. Hearing the words and catching a glimpse from the corner of his eye of the massive figure approaching like a living projectile, Yorath could not resist his reaction to try to deal with the new threat. Nevertheless, part of him still insisted upon taking revenge upon the cause of his humiliation. Therefore, he vacilated between the peace officer and the cowhand instead of moving with the deadly speed and decision he would normally have employed. Before he could select which of them to deal with first, the matter was taken from his hands in no uncertain fashion. Granted time to come into range, the peace officer drove out his big left fist. Caught on the side of the jaw, Yorath was pitched sideways in a headlong sprawl. The Colt flew from his unheeding grasp and he went down unconscious.

"I warned him not to carry a gun in my bailiwick!" Markham announced, going to pick up the short-barrelled revolver. Asking what had caused the trouble and being told that Red had tried to avoid it, he went on, "I can't blame you for defending yourself. A couple of you fellers tote this jasper down to the jailhouse for me. We'll see if a night in a cell and a fine from the judge comes morning'll make him realize we aim to have the 'No Guns In Trail End' ordinance obeyed."

"It couldn't've worked better had we told 'em what we wanted them to do," Red Blaze enthused, riding up through the darkness to where Jessica Front de Boeuf and Mark Counter were sitting horses at the edge of a trail. "Following Mr. Bruce and that skinny sod-buster was easier than it'd likely've been had Yorath been along."

"So you've seen where they're holding Trudeau?" the woman asked and the relief in her voice was genuine.

"Seen and scouted it, ma'am," the fiery haired Texan confirmed. "Trouble being, it won't be easy to pry him loose."

Not only had Jessica guessed what Red had in mind when looking from the wardrobe to her nephew, but having heard that her son's property had been collected by them, she had had a similar scheme in mind when coming to pay them a visit. However, while willing to help her, Mark had insisted that Stan Markham must be informed. Despite his aunt's obvious misgivings and disapproval, this had been done. Much to her surprise, in addition to having offered his support willingly, the town marshal had kept his questions to a minimum and avoided raising points regarding her part in the affair which could have proven embarrassing or even incriminating.

Friendship, mutual respect, trust and gratitude for help given in gaining acceptance for the "No Guns In Trail End" ordinance were not the only reasons for Markham adopting such an attitude when approached by the blond giant!

Unlike Mark, the marshal had been engaged continuously in law enforcement activities for several years. He had not needed to have the true status of the man with whom they would be in contention explained. In addition to being aware that they would be up against a ruthless and successful master criminal, he had a personal reason for giving his agreement. A friend of long standing had been murdered by Kent Bruce, but every witness was either scared from testifying, or killed, and the jury at his trial had been compelled to return a verdict of not guilty. Therefore, Markham was willing to co-operate in a scheme which might allow him to be brought to justice.

Possessing a close to encyclopedic knowledge of criminal mentality, amply backed by her own devious nature, Jessica had guessed what lay behind the kidnapping of her son. She had also formed an equally accurate assessment of how Bruce would respond if he could be led to assume this had not taken place.

To bring about the assumption, accompanied by Mark clad in Trudeau Front de Boeuf's usual attire, of a prosperous professional gambler—the requisite bulk around the mid-section being acquired by padding—the woman had selected a suitable position from which the illusion could be created. While giving the impression that she and her son were checking to ensure Bruce had arrived as stipulated with only one man, a precaution which would have been taken in any conditions, the alley she had chosen was sufficiently far away to prevent the deception being detected.

Although too far away to hear what passed between Bruce and the gangling man who met him outside the railroad depot, Jessica had deduced correctly that he was acting as a go-between for the kidnappers. Before any attempt could be made to clarify the situation by approaching her and her "son," also having been waiting close by, Markham had arrived as arranged to disarm David Yorath and lessen the chance of this being done. Unfortunately, due to having only recently come to Trail End, the marshal knew nothing about Michael Murdock. Nor was a deputy who had served with his predecessor able to say more than that the "sod-buster" always used the trail to the south-west when visiting the town.

Being deprived of what could have proved helpful information from the peace officers, Jessica had not been perturbed. The plan she had concocted offered another chance. However, having guessed that Bruce would take steps to learn the truth of the matter, she had taken into account how this would be done and made her arrangements accordingly. Agreeing that a man like Yorath would be too wary for their purposes, Red and Markham had been prepared to remove him. Collecting some friends from Texas who were willing to help without asking questions, the red head had provoked the incident and had given the marshal an excuse to take the hard-case into custody.

Using the incarceration of his bodyguard as an excuse, again as Jessica had anticipated, Bruce had notified her that he would not be available for a meeting until the following afternoon. Counting upon him considering the negotiations could not be delayed indefinitely without arousing her suspicions if there had been no kidnapping, the reply she had sent was calculated to make him uncertain over whether it had happened as arranged. Justifying her estimation of his character still further, he had elected to go with Murdock and satisfy himself on the point.

Having survived the performance of scouting missions while serving as second in command of Company "C" of the Texas Light Cavalry during the War Between The States, Red had justified his claim that he would be able to follow the two men. The task had been made easier by Bruce having waited until just after sundown before setting off. Nevertheless, he was willing to admit he was helped greatly by not being in contention against Yorath. Despite his intelligence and undoubted ability in other fields, being a city dweller, the master criminal lacked the keen perceptions of his range bred and frontier trained bodyguard. Nor, the pose of being a farmer notwithstanding, had Murdock proved any more competent in such matters.

Finding the quarter moon more of a help than a hindrance, the red haired Texan had contrived to follow his quarry to their destination without being detected. Leaving his well trained horse ground hitched by its dangling reins at a safe distance, he had been just as successful on advancing on foot to make a thorough examination of the small house and its out buildings. All were in a state of near dilapidation. Nor, with the exception of one buckboard, were the few vehicles scattered around in any better condition. Apart from half a dozen horses of varying quality, there was no livestock and, much to his relief, no dogs. Having made a mental note of everything he believed might prove of use in the rescue bid, he had collected his mount and went to tell Jessica and Mark what he had learned. They had followed him at a distance while on the south-west trail, the woman dressed as a cowhand in clothes borrowed from the blond giant and armed with her son's weapons. They awaited his return along the trail.

"I don't think either of us believed it would be *easy*!" Jessica stated, unable to control her ingrained arrogance, in response to Red's comment on rejoining them. Then, forcing a more pleasant tone into her voice, she continued, "I'm sorry, Mr. Blaze, but——!"

"That's all right, ma'am," the fiery haired Texan replied. "I've a notion how you must be feeling. Anyways, they didn't go straight up to the house. Bruce sent the sod-buster on ahead's soon as they got near, but wasn't where I could chance sneaking up and grabbing him."

"It wouldn't have done any good if you had," the woman claimed, as the cowhand paused and looked her way, as if expecting criticism for having failed to take what could have been an opportunity. "Quincy and his men wouldn't have traded Trudeau for him."

"That's about how I figured it, ma'am," Red admitted. "Quincy came out and talked to the sod-buster, who'd gone across on his lonesome, then went back in. When Quincy came out again and waved them over, instead of using the front door, they went 'round the back and must've gone in through the kitchen."

"Neither Bruce nor the sod-buster would want to let Trudeau know who they were," Jessica guessed. "I expect Quincy was sent in to have him blindfolded so he couldn't see them looking at him."

"That's how I figured it, ma'am," Red drawled.

"How's the land lie, *amigo*?" Mark inquired.

"They're holding him in the front room, at a guess," the red head replied. "Least, there's only that and the kitchen lit up. There was sacks for drapes at all the windows light showed through, so I couldn't see in. Wasn't nobody outside on guard, which's *something* and, apart from there only being three decent saddle horses in the corral, I wouldn't want to guess at how many we'll be up against."

"Three we know for sure, them having busted Cousin Tru out of the jailhouse," the blond giant stated. "Of course, there'll be Bruce and the sod-buster should they stick around."

"They won't," Jessica assessed. "Once he's satisfied they really are holding Trudeau, Bruce won't waste any time in going back to town."

"We'll figure on three for certain then and hope there isn't too many more," Mark decided. "Is there anything that might help us get up close to 'em?"

"I tell you, *amigo*, I've never seen such a runamuck place," Red asserted, after having described the layout of the farm and its immediate surroundings. "Should that jasper be living on nothing 'cept what he makes as a sod-buster, I'm not surprised he looks half-starved. Except for the rig I'll bet was used to tote your Cousin Trudeau out here, there isn't one that's whole and could be used. Would you believe there's a Chihuahua cart like you see down New Mex'-Arizona way and even that's got a wheel fallen off?"

"Is the wheel around?" the blond giant asked, thinking about the dimensions of the type of vehicle to which his companion had referred.

"It's lying where it fell off, likely, by the cart," the red head replied, intrigued by the way in which the question had been put.

"Really, nephew!" Jessica put in irritably, not knowing the blond giant as well as did the other Texan. "Does that *matter*?"

"Might do, Aunt Jessica, it just might do," Mark answered. "Something that heavy could come in pretty handy, should it be used properly."

Moving through the semi-darkness to which his vision had already adjusted, Mark Counter was alert for the slightest suggestion that his presence had been discovered by somebody in the small cluster of buildings towards which he was advancing alone and on foot. Contriving to avoid any unnecessary noise, he was conscious of the comforting weight caused by the *buscadero* gunbelt and its two ivory handled Colt Cavalry Peacemakers, once more strapped around his waist. Suspecting he would have need of the weapons, he had collected them and his Winchester Model of 1873 rifle from the office of the town marshal before setting out from Trail End. However, as things had turned out, he concluded he would not need the latter for what he had in mind.

Explaining the plan he had formulated, based on the information he had received, the blond giant had found that neither Jessica Front de Boeuf nor Red Blaze could suggest anything which might offer even as much chance of succeeding. Much to the relief of the two young Texans, the woman had decided against going any further with them. Saying she would be more of an encumbrance than help on such an expedition, she had announced her intention of returning along the trail and said she would wait for them where it passed through a small wooded area. Agreeing with her point of view, her nephew and the red head had promised they would do everything in their power to bring back her son unharmed.

Possessing considerable knowledge of the kind of work they were undertaking, the Texans had considered it inadvisable to follow the exact route to the farmhouse used by Red on his previous visit. The wisdom of taking the precaution was not long in being demonstrated. Hearing riders coming from the other direction, shortly before reaching the point at which Red had earlier left his horse, they had halted and escaped being detected themselves. Waiting until Kent Bruce and Michael Murdock had passed, they had resumed their wary approach.

Having ridden as close as they considered it would be safe to do so without being heard by the men in the cabin, the Texans dismounted and Mark tied his horse to a sturdy bush. While the big bloodbay stallion was sufficiently well trained to remain where left when only ground hitched under normal conditions, he did not care to take the chance of it being frightened into bolting by the commotion almost certain to be forthcoming, no matter how his plan turned out. With this precaution taken, the blond giant and the red head had separated so each could play the part assigned to him.

Having satisfied himself there was still no guard on the porch, Mark went around the left side of the farmhouse. He could hear voices from the front door, but was unable to either see through the sacks draped as curtains across the window or make out what was being said. Turning aside, he went in search of the vehicle upon which a vital portion of his plan depended. While doing so, regardless of the desperate nature of the situation, he wondered how it had come so far from its place of origin. Concluding it may have been brought north and abandoned on arrival by a trail drive, or sold to the farmer, he put the matter from his thoughts.

Designed to carry a sizeable load drawn by three draught oxen over rugged terrain, the Chihuahua cart was a sturdy, albeit somewhat primitive means of transportation, already being replaced in the Southwest of the United States by the four-wheeled "prairie schooner." Simplicity of design and construction were its major features, being comprised of a thick wooden bed with sides forming a box in which the load needed to be carefully balanced above the single axle.

Studying the wheel which had come from the axle and lay near the vehicle he was approaching, Mark did not underestimate the difficulty of the task he had set himself. However, he considered it would be ideally suited for his purpose provided he could make use of it as was called for by his plan.

Although equipped with iron for its box and tyre, these were the only concessions made to improving the original design. Instead of having the spokes which had become popular amongst "Anglo" users in particular, it was con-

structed from the traditional three pieces of wood forming a
solid whole. Giving a diameter of four feet, being a good
eighteen inches in width, the middle section tapered from
ten inches thick at the hub to five where the metal rim was
attached. Secured to the centrepiece by either wooden or
—more recently—metal pins, the other two portions were
cut in semicircles and of similar dimensions to form a massive bulk.

Bending over the wheel, the blond giant scrabbled
around until able to get the fingers of both hands under-
neath the edge of the centrepiece. Then, bracing himself,
he began to apply all his enormous strength to straightening
up and raising the heavy mass from the ground. Even as he
felt it moving upwards, he heard the sound of hooves approaching and a voice with drunken tones began shouting.

"Well well well, it looks like I've taken *another* pot," Trudeau Front de Boeuf announced, exuding an appearance of
joviality and complete lack of concern over his situation.
Reaching out with his manacled hands, he drew the coins
and bills from the centre of the rickety table towards him,
continuing, "It looks like this's my *lucky* day!"

"Yeah!" growled the taller of the men who had helped
the bogus United States deputy marshal to remove the big
Southron from the jailhouse in Trail End. Dressed town
fashion like his companions and also wearing a Colt Peacemaker in a fast draw holster, his tone was sour. Darting a
glance pregnant with unspoken meaning at his companions, he went on, "But *luck* can allus change!"

"So I've always heard, Ossie," Front de Boeuf conceded, his demeanour showing no discernible change despite the misgivings aroused by the cryptic comment.
"That's what makes gambling so interesting, don't you
think?"

Such was the competence displayed by Elmer Quincy

and his companions, the massive Southron had not been presented with any opportunity to escape from them. At the jailhouse, two had kept him covered with their revolvers through the bars of the door while the other entered and secured his arms from biceps to wrists with a length of rope. Knowing neither would be deterred by the possibility of injuring their companion if he had resisted within the restricted confines of the cell, he had allowed this to be done peacefully. Taken from the building to where a buckboard was waiting, he had taken the warning he was given and made no attempt to raise the alarm by shouting. Helped to climb aboard the vehicle, a sack had been placed over his head before it was set into motion.

The extemporized blindfold was not removed until, after a journey he concluded had taken him some miles from Trail End—although he had no idea in which direction—Front de Boeuf had been guided into the poorly furnished sitting-room of a dilapidated cabin built from wooden planks. The precautions against him discovering his location had not ended there. Sacks draped across the windows of every room he had been allowed to visit served to prevent him from obtaining a clue as to his whereabouts by looking outside and, when needing to "answer the calls of nature," he was made to do so in a bucket without being allowed to leave the building.

Once more having taken sufficient precautions to dissuade the big Southron from making a move against them, first attaching a set of horse hobbles to his ankles, the trio had replaced the rope around his arms with handcuffs stolen from the office of the town marshal. Accepting he could now only hope to escape if granted the most favourable circumstances, despite his hands being in front instead of behind his back, he had waited in vain for a set to occur. There had never been a moment when he was watched by just one of his abductors. Furthermore, although he had not put in an appearance, there had been a voice and other indications that a fourth man was on the premises some of the time.

Although the big Southron had been informed that a demand for a ransom of three thousand dollars had been sent to await the arrival of his mother at their hotel, whereupon he would be set free once the money had been delivered, he had suspected this was merely an inducement to keep him from trying to escape. Like Jessica, he had guessed who was behind the kidnapping. Wanting to confirm his supposition, in case he should survive and be able to take revenge, he had adopted a means which he hoped would do so. Aware that tongues were frequently loosened during a game of cards, as well as when liquor flowed— which it did not in the cabin—while having lunch, he had suggested they pass the time playing poker and they had agreed.

In spite of having been unable to employ any of the cheating methods at which he was adept, due to his wrists being manacled, Front de Boeuf possessed the skill of a successful professional gambler. This and a favourable run of the cards had enabled him to win consistently from his less experienced opponents. However, none of them had been tricked into saying anything which would implicate Kent Bruce in the kidnapping.

On the point of suggesting the game be brought to an end, having noticed his captors were growing increasingly resentful over their continued losses, the big Southron had heard two horses approaching. Although the sack had been placed over his head, he had known when Quincy was summoned into the kitchen. The door had been closed, preventing him from making out what was being said, but he had drawn an accurate conclusion from the conversation which had taken place. Returning after the visitors had taken their departure, the bogus peace officer had told his companions their money had arrived. When asked by Front de Boeuf how soon he would be set free in that case, Quincy had replied this would be done in the morning, and demanded the next pot was dealt.

Ever susceptible to atmosphere, the big Southron had soon detected a change coming over his captors. Nevertheless, they had continued to play until his comment on taking another pot provoked the cryptic comment from Ossie. This increased his belief that he was not to be let leave the cabin alive. Having received their payment from Bruce, they would have no intention of letting him survive to search for them and avenge his abduction.

Before anything further could be said, there was an interruption!

Hooves sounded, approaching from the same direction as the earlier riders, but this time of a single horse!

The animal was brought to a halt a short distance from the front of the cabin, then a voice with the slurred timbre suggesting the newcomer was drunk began to bellow.

"Hey there in the house!" boomed the voice, its accent Texan. "Susie-Mae, Winnie, Josey-fine, come on out here. It's your good ole *amigo*, Pockets Hoscroft from Tennyson, pride of the Lone Star State callin' with the rest of the Hide 'N' Horn trail crew close behind all comin' a-courting like we did while you was living in town."

"There's only the one out there!" Ossie reported, having darted with gun in hand to peer cautiously through the front window while his companions had drawn their Colts and covered the big Southron. "I can down him from here real easy!"

"The hell you will!" Quincy refused savagely. "Didn't you hear the beef-head son-of-a-bitch say the rest of his god-damned trail crew're close behind?"

"I don't see hide nor hair of 'em!" Ossie claimed, but lowered the hand he had raised to open the window.

"How far can you see on a night like this?" the bogus peace officer countered. He too was surprised by the visit, but not suspicious. News of how Trail End had been cleaned up had reached him and he assumed, as frequently happened, this had included the closing of all the brothels. Although somewhat further away than he would have expected, he considered it possible that one might have been relocated in the vicinity of the farm. "Go out and tell him he's come to the wrong place. Get over to the door and stop him seeing in here, Gil. But don't neither of you start shooting, else we'll have the rest of the bastards swarming down on us like stirred up hornets."

Completing the shouted introduction, which Mark Counter had assured him would produce the effect they desired, Red Blaze swung from his double girthed Texas saddle. He was somewhat further away from the cabin than he would have liked, but he considered it was advisable not to go closer for reasons similar to those that had caused the blond giant to tie up the bloodbay stallion. There was, he told himself wryly, an even greater danger of his big claybank mount being spooked into bolting as he would be compelled to rely upon only ground hitching it.

Watching the front door of the building open and a man step out, the fiery haired Texan noticed it was pushed until only just ajar before he could see the interior. Realizing why this had been done, he allowed the split-end reins to slip from his fingers. Then, making sure he kept his hands clear of the forward pointing walnut butts of the Colt Cavalry Model Peacemakers in the low cavalry-twist draw holsters of his gunbelt, he strolled forward with a gait complimentary to the drunken way in which he had spoken.

"Howdy there, young feller!" Ossie greeted, forcing himself to sound more amiable than he was feeling. Starting to cross the porch with his gun-filled right hand concealed behind his back, he scanned the terrain beyond the caller. "You've come to the wrong place. There ain't no gals here, they're out along the main trail maybe another mile or so."

"Why now, that just cain't be so!" Red protested, retaining the suggestion of intoxication in his voice and posture as he kept walking. Measuring the distance separating him from the approaching man, who he hoped to render *hors de combat* silently when close enough, he continued, "This's where me 'n' the rest of the crew was told to come. I bet you 'n' your *amigos* 're inside having fun with all those hot-assed lil gals and don't wanna share none of 'em with us."

"That just ain't so, young feller," Ossie denied, trying to sound like a church-going farmer confronted by such a mistake and straining his ears in an attempt to discover how close the unwanted caller's companions might be. "I tell you this's the wrong pl—!"

A crash and the crackle of planks being shattered came from the left side of the cabin and brought the explanation to an end!

Unfortunately, despite having expected such a commotion, Red was still well beyond reaching distance of his objective!

To make matters worse, although startled, the man from the cabin glanced around briefly then returned his gaze to the fiery haired Texan, starting to bring the concealed right hand from behind his back!

Listening to the conversation taking place in front of the cabin, the blond giant was unable to see the speakers. However, he knew Red was aware of his intentions and would be ready to take action. Hoping his cousin had drawn the correct conclusions from the names used by his *amigo* on riding up, he gave a surging heave. Raising the heavy wheel above his head, he strode forward a couple of steps and hurled it at the window. His aim was off and, instead of striking the glass, the iron bound rim of the circular pieces of timber hit the wall to one side. Nevertheless, this produced what was probably an even more dramatic and effective result.

Allowed to become warped and brittle by the neglect of successive owners, the planks could not withstand such an impact. To the accompaniment of a cacophony of snapping wood, the wheel burst through and caused the half of the wall beyond the window to fall inwards. Hearing startled exclamations from the room, Mark brought out his Colts with the swiftly flowing movement which characterized a gun fighter of the first water. Filled with anxiety for the welfare of his cousin, he leapt towards the gaping hole he had created.

Like every experienced poker player, Trudeau Front de Boeuf had excellent control over his emotions. Therefore, he had shown none of the elation which was aroused by hearing the obviously Texan visitor mention Pockets Hoscroft, Tennyson and the Hide And Horn "trail crew." The latter were, in fact, the names of a town and a saloon, and all three had been involved in the last meeting he had had with his cousin.

Even possessing such knowledge, the big Southron was almost as startled as Elmer Quincy and Gil by the means selected to create a distraction!

Almost!

But not quite!

As a precaution against being seen by the big Southron, being unaware that the trio had decided to kill him instead of letting him be set free on receiving the ransom, Michael Murdock had insisted that he was always seated with his back to the kitchen door. While this saved him from being struck by the section of the wall which was caved in by the

massive wheel, unfortunately he was not alone in the
escape. Quincy was seated at the right side of the table and
Gil stood by the door.

Regardless of being alarmed by the totally unexpected
turn of events, neither the bogus peace officer nor the
shorter of his companions was frozen into more than a momentary immobility!

Spitting out a profanity, Quincy began to lift his Colt
and thrust himself from the chair!

Releasing the handle he was holding, ready to leave
hurriedly if Ossie needed help, the third of the abductors
swung around and also started to turn his gun towards their
captive!

Suspecting why the approaching man had kept the hand
concealed, Red responded to the threat. His instinct also
warned that, the clothing of a town dweller notwithstanding, he was up against a sufficiently competent gun handler
to be very dangerous. Aware of his own limitations in that
field, he took what he considered to be the most suitable
counter measures. Turning the palm of his right hand outwards, he closed it around the walnut grips and twisted the
off side long barrelled Peacemaker from its holster. While
doing so, he flung himself in a dive to the left.

The evasion was only just in time!

Flame lashed from the muzzle of the Colt brought
around by Ossie. Its bullet cut the air just above the
Texan's descending body. Landing on his side, Red rolled
to his back and slanted the Peacemaker upwards. Although
he had drawn back the hammer with his right thumb and
inserted his forefinger through the triggerguard the moment
the barrel cleared the lip of the holster and turned away
from him, he did not continue to employ this method of
operating the mechanism. Instead, having dispatched his
first shot, he brought across and used the heel of his
cupped left hand to return the hammer to the firing posi-

tion. On being released, the trigger being kept depressed, it flew forward to discharge the cartridge waiting in the uppermost chamber of the cylinder.

Fanning was the fastest way to fire a single action revolver, which needed to be cocked manually, but it was not conducive to great accuracy. However, this proved to be no disadvantage to Red under the circumstances. Sending out shot after shot in very rapid succession, he angled them slightly apart. Before Ossie could correct his aim, being dazzled by his own and the repeated muzzle flashes from the gun of his intended victim, he was caught in the chest by the fourth and fifth .45 calibre bullets. The sixth just missed him as he was pitched backwards, dying, to the ground.

"Getting those three jaspers to grab off that big feller like you did was real slick, boss," Michael Murdock praised, as he and Kent Bruce were riding along the trail towards the small area of woodland through which it passed.

"Maybe not slick enough," the master criminal replied pensively, jolted from his thoughts on what he had learned from the kidnappers of Trudeau Front de Boeuf. "That's 'Coeur de Lion' at your place all right. So what the hell was his mother up to trying to make me think he was with her?"

"She was scared of letting you know she was on her lonesome," the go-between suggested.

"*Scared*?" Bruce snorted. "*She* wouldn't even be scared by the crack of doom and knowing the Day of Judgement was coming. No, there was more to it than that."

"Aw, boss!" Murdock protested, ever the sycophant. "She couldn't've figured it was you's fixed it for him to be grabbed off."

"The hell she couldn't!" Bruce denied, with a mixture of heat and concern. "It didn't strike me until Quincy mentioned 'Coeur de Lion' had a cousin even bigger than him in town, but she'd have come straight to me for help if she hadn't guessed what was doing."

"What're you going to do, boss?" the go-between inquired.

"It all depends upon *her*," the master criminal replied, but did not consider it advisable to tell his companion he had no intention of leaving such a dangerous person as he knew "Jessica Coeur de Lion" to be, alive under the circumstances. "God damn Yorath for losing his temper and getting thrown into jail. If I lose what she's got for me because of it, I'll——!"

The delivery of the threat was brought to an end by the sound of shooting in the direction from which the two men had come!

"That's at my place!" Murdock stated, as he and his employer looked around while reining their horses to a halt.

"I *know* it is!" Bruce snarled, thinking fast and drawing satisfaction from realizing he would be able to find his way back to the town by following the trail and no longer needed guiding. "Go back and find out what's happening!"

"Maybe they've shot him now they've got your money, 'stead of doing what you said," the go-between suggested, knowing the arrangement had been for the kidnappers to hold their captive at his farm until the actual ransom had passed via him to the master criminal.

"Do as I told you!" Bruce hissed viciously, but refrained from expressing his belief that the shooting had occurred outside the building. "Move, god damn you!"

"S—Sure, boss!" the 'sod-buster' assented, albeit reluctantly, alarmed by the way in which he had been addressed. "W—What'll I do when I've found out?"

"Come to town as fast as you can and tell *me*!" the

master criminal instructed over his shoulder, having already set his mount into motion.

Riding away from the man he had hired to supply local knowledge and facilities, Bruce was concerned solely with giving thought to his immediate future. He was becoming increasingly and disturbingly aware that he was no longer in an area where he could exert influence. Because of the precautions demanded by "Jessica Coeur de Lion," justifiable as they had been when dealing with him, he had only a single man upon whom he could depend for protection. Even David Yorath had been so stupidly inconsiderate as to get thrown in jail for becoming involved in an unnecessary brawl and carrying a revolver in defiance of the "No Guns In Trail End" civic ordinance.

The situation was hardly conducive to peace of mind, especially when in contention against such a completely unscrupulous and deadly woman!

One asset which had always stood the master criminal in good stead was his ability to judge when to cut and run. Regardless of the profits which he felt sure would accrue from the information he had hired Jessica to acquire, being convinced she would have upheld her reputation where such things were concerned, he concluded the safest course was to forget it and make for a place offering him a secure sanctuary as quickly as possible. Once there, aware that he would never be able to travel freely or even rest safely while she lived and sought vengeance, he could make arrangements for her to be killed.

Thinking of his escape, Bruce entered the gloom caused by the trail passing between the trees and undergrowth of the woodland. A man raised in the range country would have drawn an appropriate conclusion from the way his horse tossed its head and, snuffling the air, gave a snort which was answered in kind from the shadows on the left side of the trail. Being a city dweller, whose love of luxury and easy living led to using a vehicle instead of sitting a saddle when travelling, he failed to appreciate the significance of such equine behaviour.

The master criminal was not left long in ignorance of the danger!

"Unless I'm doing it, Kent-*darling*!" announced a feminine voice from a distinctly masculine seeming shape, which lunged from the bushes close to where the response of the second horse originated. "I just *loathe* double dealing!"

Brought from his reverie by the words, their accent being that of a well bred Southron and imbued by a chilling vicious timbre, Bruce was only given just enough time to realize who was addressing him!

Even as the understanding sent terror flooding through the master criminal, but before he could start to think of escaping what he knew instinctively was coming, it was too late!

Holding her son's Greener whipit gun at waist level in both hands, Jessica Front de Boeuf squeezed the triggers in rapid succession. Using such a specialized weapon at close quarters, there was no need for her to take a more careful aim. With a double bellow which came so close it formed almost a single sound, two jets of flame erupted from the shortened side by side barrels of the shotgun. Belched out ahead of the fiery muzzle blast, eighteen .32 calibre buckshot balls spread like an opening fan as they passed through the air in their upwards angled flight.

Chance rather than deliberate intention caused the separate segments of moulded lead to miss the horse. However, several struck the rider in his head and torso. Shying from the awesome commotion, the animal was further thrown off balance by the involuntary actions of the stricken master criminal. Knocked sideways by the multiple impacts, his feet remained in the stirrup irons for long enough to cause his mount to follow him down and roll over him. Several of his ribs were broken, but he was already dead and past feeling the crushing pressure against the unyielding ground.

Taking her right hand from the butt of the whipit gun, Jessica drew her son's Colt Pocket Pistol of Navy Calibre —sometimes erroneously called the "Model of 1853" and a five-shot revolver regardless of its name—from where she was carrying it tucked into the left side of her borrowed trousers' waistband. Not until she was once more holding a fully loaded weapon did she walk towards where Bruce was sprawling limply on the trail and his horse was scrambling to its feet. She did not believe it would be needed where the master criminal was concerned, but wanted to be prepared if the man who had acted as his guide should put in an appearance. The precaution was unnecessary. Although she did not know, having heard the blast of the shotgun, Michael Murdock decided against carrying out even the first part of the orders he had been given and was already taking flight.

"What a *fool* you were, Kent-darling," the woman remarked in a matter-of-fact tone, gazing with neither remorse nor revulsion at the motionless human body from which she had just taken life. Even without having deduced the intentions he had where her future was concerned, she would not have hesitated to kill him under the circumstances. "You could have avoided *this* and made so much money from what I had for you. But then, I always did hear you were *greedy.* It's just a pity I had to finish you off outright. I'd have *much* preferred to have you alive, so you could really learn what suffering meant if any harm has befallen my boy."

Bellowing, "*Cave adsum*!", to provide an indication of his position in the room for the benefit of his cousin outside,

Front de Boeuf discarded the slothful way in which he had behaved since being forced to leave the cell. Interlacing his fingers, he rose with great rapidity for one of his bulk. Sending his chair and the table flying, he pivoted towards Quincy. Lashing around, impelled by all the power of his enormously muscular body, the interlocked hands crashed under the chin of the bogus peace officer. There was an audible pop as the neck was broken by the impact. Thrown bodily across the room, his head flopping limply, Quincy was dead before he crashed into the right side wall and bounced from it to the floor.

Swiftly though the big Southron had moved, he knew he was still far from being out of danger!

Already Gil was turning by the door and there was no way Front de Boeuf could cross the room in time to prevent him shooting!

Plunging through the gap he had made, Mark took in the situation with a hurried glance. Having heard the motto of the Front de Boeuf family had helped him fix the approximate position of his cousin before he entered. His scrutiny soon informed him where he must devote his attention.

For all that, it was a *very* close thing!

In fact, if Gil had not been distracted by the arrival of the blond giant, his plan might have failed to produce the desired result!

Seeing the enormous figure, the man at the door inadvertently turned his Colt away from its alignment. The margin was so slight that, in passing, the bullet cut off a lock of Front de Boeuf's brown hair. Gil was not allowed to try again. Right, left, right, left, the ivory handled Peacemakers in Mark's skilled hands roared alternately from waist level. In spite of this, every bullet flew true and any one of them would have been fatal. Torso perforated by the lead, which had passed through to tear his back asunder, Gil went down with the revolver flying from his lifeless grasp.

"Whooee, Cousin Mark!" Front de Boeuf ejaculated, walking over and starting to go through the pockets of the man he had killed. "Am I pleased to see *you*!"

"Something told me you might be," the blond giant replied dryly, then he raised his voice. "Are you all right, *amigo*?"

"Got a bruised hip where I lit down on it," Red replied cheerfully from outside the cabin. "But I'm in a whole heap better shape than the other feller, 'cepting I'm going to chase after that god-damned claybank of mine. He's lit out on me."

"You should've tied him up like I did my bloodbay," Mark answered.

"I never thought of *that*!" the fiery haired Texan claimed and, despite knowing there would not have been the levity if things had gone wrong, went on, "You manage your end all right?"

"I'm fine, Red!" Front de Boeuf announced, then turned his gaze to his cousin and straightened up. "Wouldn't you know this bastard would forget to bring the keys for these handcuffs?"

"We'll cut them off for you," the blond giant suggested. "But you'll have to pay Stan Markham to replace them."

"I'll do that with pleasure," Front de Boeuf promised and meant what he said for once. "What's more, I'll have momma tell Aunt Cornelia how you saved my life the next time she writes home."

While making the offer, the big Southron watched for any reaction it might elicit from his cousin. The woman to whom he referred was their aged and very wealthy maiden aunt. Despite believing she would leave her considerable fortune to them, having been robbed by Jessica, Cornelia Front de Boeuf had changed her will in favour of Mark.

Learning of this, the beautiful and unscrupulous woman had already made and been thwarted in an attempt to have the blond giant killed. Although the change and its cause had not been circulated amongst other members of the family, Front de Boeuf was hoping to discover if the facts were known to his cousin. From what he could detect, he assumed they had not.

"There's no call for that," the blond giant protested, not realizing he was being subjected to a quest for information. "Hell, Tru, the world'd be a sorry sort of place happen members of a family can't count on each other when they're in trouble."

PART FOUR

Unfortunately, space does not permit us to include one of the Ysabel Kid's adventures in this volume. However, in addition to his other claims to fame, he acquired a reputation for being a pleasing singer.[1] Therefore, in response to numerous requests from members of the J.T. EDSON APPRECIATION SOCIETY, we have decided to use the remaining pages to record the songs he has sung in various of our other works and a couple which he favoured but have not yet appeared in print. Regrettably, we are unable to supply the music for any of these. We had hoped to have this produced by a musical associate from our "spiritual home," the White Lion Hotel in Melton Mowbray. Hearing us give voice to the first, declaring he had no wish to be turned tone deaf, he disappeared and has not been seen since.

There are in all probability more verses for the first two songs, but we have been unable to learn them.

1. To whet the appetites of new readers who have yet to make the acquaintance of the Ysabel Kid we have given details of his family background and special qualifications in: *Appendix Three*. J.T.E.

He's the fastest gun in Texas and the bravest of them all,
On a street, you'd walk right by him 'cause he isn't very
       tall,
Comes trouble, he's the boldest, fights like a Comanche
       Dog,
He's from the Rio Hondo country and his name is Dusty
       Fog.

* * *

I saw a big-pig Yankee marshal a'coming down the street,
He's got two big pistols in his hands and looks fierce
       enough to eat,
Oh big-pig Yankee stay away, keep right away from me,
I'm just a lil boy from Texas and scared as I can be.

* * *

A Yankee rode down into Texas,
A mean kind of cuss and real sly,
He fell in love with sweet Rosemary-Jo,
Then turned and told her, "Goodbye."

So Rosemary-Jo told her tough pappy,
Who yelled, "Why *hombre*, that's bad,
In tears you done left my Rosemary-Jo,
No Yankee can make my gal sad."

So he whipped out his trusty ole hawg-legs,
At which he wasn't never slow,
When the Yankee done saw him a-coming,
He knowed it was time for to go.

He jumped on his fast-running speed horse,
And fogged like hell to the West,
Then Rosemary-Jo got left her a fortune,
He come back and said he loved her best.

"Oh no!" she cried in a minute,
"I love me a Texan so sweet,
And I'm headed down to ole Dallas town,
My sweet Texan cowhand to meet."

So the Yankee rode down to the border,
He met his ole pal, Bandy Parr,
Who run with the carpetbaggers,
And a meeting they held in a bar.

Rosemary-Jo for word to her pappy,
He straddled his strawberry roan,
And said, "From that ornery critter,
I'll save Rosemary-Jo who's my own."

Now the Yankee got called out in Dallas,
Met her pappy out on the square,
His draw was too slow and as far as I know,
The Yankee's still lying out there.

* * *

It was on a Wednesday night, the moon was shining bright,
When they robbed the Glendale train,
And the folks they all did say, for many miles away,
'Twas the outlaws, Frank and Jesse James.
Chorus:

Jesse had a wife who'd mourn all her life,
With children who'd be brave,
But the dirty little coward's'd shot down Mr. Howard,
Had laid Jesse James in his grave.

It was Jesse's brother Frank's robbed the Galatin bank,
And carried off the money from the town,
And in that very place, they had a little race,

'Cause they shot Captain Sheets to the ground.
Chorus:

Jesse was real kind, a friend to the poor,
He could never see nobody suffer pain,
He stole from the rich to give to the poor,
That's why he robbed the Glendale train.
Chorus:

They went to a crossing not very far from there,
Again they took a train,
And the agent on his knees, he delivered up the keys,
To those outlaws, Frank and Jesse James.
Chorus:

It was on a Saturday and Jesse was at home,
Talking with his family so brave,
When a man came along, like a thief in the night
And laid poor old Jesse in his grave.
Chorus:

The people held their breath when they heard of Jesse's
death,
They wondered how he ever came to die,
It was at a traitor's hand, a member of his band,
Who had shot poor old Jesse on the sly.
Chorus:

They call him Robert Ford, that dirty little coward,
And I wonder how he does feel,
For he'd eaten Jesse's bread and slept in Jesse's bed,
Then snuck up and shot Jesse from behind.
Chorus:

Jesse went to his rest with one hand upon his breast,
But the Devil won't be sitting on his knee,
He was born one day in the County of Clay,
And he came of a solitary race.
Chorus:

* * *

Folks feud down in Jack County, Texas,
Worse than any other place in the world,
But, 'stead of looking to his gun, Ole Bert Taggert's son,
Had soft thoughts for Tobe Wilson's girl.

Young Bart had grown up in Jack County,
His paw raised him to live by what's thought right,
Had him sworn on the morn of the day he was born,
To shoot every Wilson on sight.

"Powder and shot for the Wilsons,
Don't even spare a hair on their heads,"
Old Bart Taggert cried as he laid down and died,
With Young Bart stood right by his bed.

Young Bart took that oath from his pappy,
He swore he would kill all that clan,
His head was in a whirl for love of the girl,
But he loaded up his six-shooting gun.

All over the rangeland he wandered,
This son of a Jack County man,
With blood in his eye and a Colt at his thigh,
He went looking for Tobe Wilson's clan.

Shots ringing out through the woodland,
Shots thundering down on the breeze,
Until Bart Taggert's son stood with smoke in his gun,

And the Wilsons were all down on their knees.

The fame of old Jack County's feuding,
Has gone far and wide o'er the world,
Since Bart Taggert's son wiped a clan out to a man,
But he brought back Tobe Wilson's girl.

We would like to point out that there may be changes in the words from other versions of these songs which have appeared in our works. This is because the Ysabel Kid was a natural and untrained singer, so never felt the need to be restricted to repeating the lyrics identically.

Appendix One

Following his enrolment in the Army of the Confederate States,[1] by the time he reached the age of seventeen, Dustine Edward Marsden "Dusty" Fog had won promotion in the field to the rank of captain and was put in command of the Company "C", Texas Light Cavalry.[2] At the head of them through the campaign in Arkansas, he had earned the reputation for being an exceptionally capable military raider and a worthy contemporary for the South's other leading exponents of what would later become known as "commando" raids,[3] Turner Ashby and John Singleton "the Grey Ghost" Mosby.[4] In addition to preventing a pair of pro-Union fanatics from starting an Indian uprising which would have decimated much of Texas[5] and thwarting a Yankee plot to employ a variant of mustard gas in the conflict,[6] he had supported Belle "the Rebel spy" Boyd on two of her most dangerous assignments.[7]

At the conclusion of the War Between The States, Dusty became segundo of the great OD Connected ranch in Rio Hondo County, Texas. Its owner and his maternal uncle, General Jackson Baines "Ole Devil" Hardin, C.S.A., had been crippled in a riding accident,[8] placing much responsibility—including handling an important mision, with the future relations between the United States and Mexico dependent upon the outcome[9]—upon his young shoulders. After helping to gather horses to replenish the ranch's depleted *remuda*,[10] he was sent to assist Colonel Charles Goodnight[11] on the trail drive to Fort Sumner, New Mexico, which had done much to help the Lone Star State recover from the impoverished conditions left by the War.[12] With that achieved, he had been equally successful in helping Goodnight convince other ranchers it would be possible to drive large herds of longhorn cattle to the railroad in Kansas.[13]

Having proven himself to be a first class cowhand, Dusty went on to become acknowledged as a very competent trail boss,[14] roundup captain [15] and town taming lawman.[16] Competing in the first Cochise County Fair against a number of well known exponents of fast drawing and accurate shooting, he won the title, "Fastest Gun In The West."[17] In later years, following his marriage to Lady Winifred Amelia "Freddie Woods" Besgrove-Woodstole, he became a noted diplomat.[18]

Dusty never found his lack of stature an impediment to his achievements. In fact, as recorded in other volumes as well as in the present narrative, he occasionally found it helped him achieve a purpose.[19] To supplement his natural strength,[20] he had taught himself to be completely ambidextrous.[21] Possessing perfectly attuned reflexes, he could draw either, or both, his Colts—whether the 1860 Army Model[22] or their improved "descendant," the fabled 1873 Model "Peacemaker"[23]—with lightning speed and shoot with great accuracy. Ole Devil Hardin's "valet", Tommy Okasi was Japanese and a trained *samaurai* warrior.[24] From him, along with the General's "granddaughter", Elizabeth "Betty" Hardin,[25] Dusty learned *ju jitsu* and *karate*. Neither form of unarmed combat had received the publicity both would be given in later years and were little known in the Western Hemisphere at that time. Therefore, Dusty found the knowledge very useful when he had to fight bare-handed against larger, heavier and stronger men.

1. Details of some of Dusty Fog's activities prior to his enrolment are given in: *Part Five. "A Time For Improvization, Mr. Blaze," J.T.'s Hundredth*.

2. Told in: *You're In Command Now, Mr. Fog*.

3. The first "commandos" were groups of irregular South African forces which gave a great deal of trouble with their "hit and run" tactics to the British Army which was opposing them in the Boer War.

4. Told in: *The Big Gun; Under The Stars And Bars, Part One, "The Futility Of War," The Fastest Gun In Texas*—a somewhat "pin the tail on the donkey" title changed, without consulting us, by our first publisher in place of the one we had given the manuscript—and *Kill Dusty Fog*.

5. Told in: *The Devil Gun*.

6. Told in: *A Matter Of Honour*.

7. Told in: *The Colt And The Sabre* and *The Rebel Spy*.

7a. Other incidents in the career of Belle "the Rebel Spy" Boyd are given in: *The Bloody Border; Back To The Bloody Border; The Hooded Riders; The Bad Bunch; Set A-Foot; To Arms! To Arms! In Dixie!; The South Will Rise Again; Part Eight, "Affair Of Honour", J.T.'s Hundredth; The Remittance Kid; The Whip And The War Lance* and *Part Five, "The Butcher's Fiery End", J.T.'s Ladies*.

8. Told in: *Part Three, "The Paint," The Fastest Gun In Texas*.

8a. Further details of General Hardin's career are given in the *Ole Devil Hardin* and Civil War series. His sobriquet had arisen as a result of the way, in his youth, he had enhanced the Mephistophelian aspects of his features and because his contemporaries claimed he was "a lil ole devil for a fight."

9. Told in: *The Ysabel Kid*; our original title being changed from *Dusty Fog* by our first publishers.

10. Told in: *.44 Calibre Man* and *A Horse Called Mogollon*.

11. Although acknowledged as a master cattleman, Charles Goodnight never served in the army. The title "Colonel" was honorary, given as a tribute to his ability as a fighting man and leader by his fellow Texans. Later in life, Dusty Fog was given the same prefix for possessing similar qualities.

11a. In addition to the titles in *Footnotes 12* and *13*, Colonel Goodnight makes "guest" *appearances in: Sidewinder; Part One, "The Half Breed", The Half Breed*, its "expansion", *White Indians* and *The Man From Texas*.

12. Told in: *Goodnight's Dream* (U.S.A. Bantam edition, July, 1974,

re-titled, *The Floating Outfit*, despite our already having published a book with this title) and *From Hide And Horn*.

13. Told in: *Set Texas Back On Her Feet* (Changed in the U.S.A. Berkley October, 1978, edition to, *Viridian's Trail*, but subsequently returned by them to its original title).

14. Told in: *Trail Boss*, our first published work.

15. Told in: *The Man From Texas* (Changed from our original and, in our opinion, far more apt title, *Roundup Captain*, by our first publishers.)

16. Told in: *Quiet Town*, *The Making Of A Lawman*, *The Trouble Busters*, *The Gentle Giant*, *The Small Texan* and *The Town Tamers*.

17. Told in: *Gun Wizard*.

18. Members of the Hardin, Fog and Blaze clan and of the Besgrove-Woodstole family with whom we have been in contact cannot, or *will not* say why Lady Winifred Amelia elected to live in the United States and adopted the alias, "Freddie Woods". How she first became acquainted with Dusty Fog is recorded in: *The Making Of A Lawman*.

19. Examples are given in: *Kill Dusty Fog!*; Chapter One, "A Case of Mistaken Identity", *The Texan*; Part One, "The Schoolteacher", *The Hard Riders*; it's "expansion", *Master Of Triggernometry* and Part One, "The Phantom Of Gallup Creek", *The Floating Outfit*.

20. Examples of Dusty Fog exhibiting his exceptional muscular development and strength are recorded in: *The Peacemakers* and *Master Of Triggernometry*.

21. The ambidextrous prowess was in part hereditary. It was possessed and exploited with equal success by Dusty's grandson, Alvin Dustine "Cap" Fog, who also inherited the physique of a Hercules in miniature. Utilizing these traits helped him to become the youngest man ever to attain the rank of captain in the Texas Rangers and become acknowledged as one of the finest combat pistol shots of his generation. See the Alvin Dustine "Cap" Fog series for further details.

22. Although the military sometimes claimed it was easier to kill a sailor than a soldier, perhaps a trifle tongue in cheek, the weight factor of the respective weapons had been responsible for the decision by the United States' Navy to adopt a revolver of .36 calibre while the Army employed the heavier .44. The weapon would be carried on the belt of a seaman and not—handguns having originally and primarily developed for single-handed use by cavalry—on the person or saddle of a soldier who would be doing much of his travelling and fighting on the back of a horse. Therefore, .44 became known as the "Army" and .36 the "Navy" calibre.

23. Introduced in 1873 as the Colt Model P "Single Action Army" revolver—although its original production calibre was .45 and not .44—but more popularly referred to as the "Peacemaker", it was manufactured continuously until it was taken out of the line in 1941 to make way for more modern weapons required in World War II. Over three hundred and fifty thousand were produced, in practically every handgun calibre—with the exception of the .41 and .44 Magnums, which were not developed

until after manufacture had been stopped—from .22 Short Rimfire to .476 Eley. However, the majority fired a cartridge of either .45 of .44.40. The latter, given the distinguishing title, "Frontier Model", handled the same ammunition as was used by the Winchester Model of 1873 rifle and carbine.

23a. The Peacemaker was offered in barrel lengths of from three inches in the "Storekeeper" Model, which did not have an extractor rod, to sixteen inches for the so-called, "Buntline Special". An attachable metal "skeleton" butt stock was available for the latter, allowing it to be converted into an extemporized carbine. The main barrel lengths were: "Civilian", four and threequarter inches; "Artillery", five and a half and "Cavalry", first to be issued, seven and a half.

23b. Popular demand, said to have been caused by the upsurge of action-escapism-adventure Western series on television, brought the Peacemaker back into production in 1965 and it is still in the line. For the first time, the Colt Patent Firearms Manufacturing Company issued a Model—albeit with only a twelve inch barrel—which they called the "Buntline Special". This was in response to public demand, aroused by the use of such a weapon by actor Hugh O'Brien, star of the *Wyatt Earp* television series.

23c. We consider at best specious—at worst, a snobbish attempt to "put down" the myth and legends of the Old West—the often repeated assertion that the gun fighters of that era could not "hit a barn door at twenty yards". While willing to concede the average person then, as now, would not have had much skill at handling a handgun, knowing his life depended upon it, the professional *pistolero* on either side of the law expended time, money and effort to acquire competence. Furthermore, such a man did not carry a revolver to indulge in shooting at anything except close range. He wanted a readily accessible *weapon* which would incapacitate an enemy, preferably with the first shot, at close quarters. With the exception of .22 calibre handguns intended for casual pleasure shooting, specially adapted for Olympic style target matches, or the Remington XP 100—one of which makes its appearance in, *Case Two, "A Voice From The Past", The Lawmen Of Rockabye County*—designed for "varmint" hunting at long range, or in the hands of a very proficient modern exponent of "combat pistol" work, a handgun is a *defensive*, not an *offensive* weapon. Any Old West gun fighter, or modern peace officer, expecting to have to shoot at distances beyond twenty or so feet would take the precaution of arming himself with a shotgun or a rifle.

24. The name "Tommy Okasi" is an Americanized corruption of the one given by the man in question, who had had to leave Japan for reasons the author is not allowed to divulge, when rescued by a ship under the command of General Hardin's father from a derelict vessel in the China Sea.

25. The members of the Hardin, Fog and Blaze clan with whom we have attempted to discuss the matter flatly refuse to make any statement upon the exact relationship between Elizabeth "Betty" and General Hardin. She appears in: *Part Four, "It's Our Turn To Improvise, Miss Blaze", J.T.'s*

Ladies; Kill Dusty Fog!; The Bad Bunch, McGraw's Inheritance; Master of Triggernometry, Part Two, "The Quartet", The Half Breed, The Rio Hondo War and *Gunsmoke Thunder* (Another example of an unexplained title change by our first publisher, our choice having been, *Comanche Blake's Gal*.)

Appendix Two

With his exceptional good looks and magnificent physical development, Mark Counter presented the kind of appearance which many people expected of Dusty Fog. It was a fact of which they took advantage should the need arise[1] and, once was almost the cause of the blond giant being subjected to a murder attempt although the small Texan was intended as the victim.[2]

Whilst serving under the command of General Bushrod Sheldon during the War Between The States, Mark's merits as an efficient and courageous officer had been overshadowed by his unconventional taste in uniforms. Always a dandy, coming from a wealthy family and, later, given independent means in the will of a maternal maiden aunt, had allowed him to indulge his whims. His selection of a skirtless tunic, for example, had been much copied by the young bloods of the Confederate States' Army—including, although they had not yet met, Captain Dusty Fog—despite considerable opposition and disapproval on the part of hide-bound senior officers.

When peace came, Mark followed Sheldon into Mexico to fight for Emperor Maximilian. There, he had met Dusty and the Ysabel Kid, helping to accomplish the former's mission. On returning to Texas, he had been invited to join the OD Connected ranch and become a founder member of its elite "floating outfit".[3] Knowing his father and his two elder brothers could run the great R Over C ranch in the Big Bend country without needing his aid—and suspecting life would be more exciting in the company of his *amigos* —he accepted.

An expert cowhand, Mark was known as Dusty's right bower.[4] He had also gained acclaim by virtue of his enormous strength and ability in a roughhouse brawl. However, due to being so much in the company of the Rio Hondo gun wizard, his full potential as a gun fighter tended to be given less attention. Men who were competent to judge such matters stated he was second only to Dusty in speed and accuracy.

Many women found Mark's handsome appearance irresistible, including Miss Martha "Calamity Jane" Canary.[5] Nevertheless, in his younger days, only one, the lady outlaw, Belle Starr[6]—held his heart. It was not until several years after Belle's death that—we suspect due to matchmaking by Elizabeth "Betty" Raybold, nee Hardin—he courted and married Dawn Sutherland, who he had first met on the trail drive led by Colonel Charles Goodnight to Fort Sumner, New Mexico. The discovery of vast oil deposits on the ranch they purchased brought added wealth to them and forms a major part of the income for the present day members of the family. Three descendants of Mark, each of whom inherited his looks and physique, achieved fame on their own account.[7]

Recent biographical details received from the current head of the family, Andrew Mark "Big Andy" Counter establishes that Mark was descended on his mother's side from Sir Reginald Front de Boeuf, notorious as master of Torquilstone Castle in Medieval England[8] and who lived up to the family motto, *Cave Adsum*.[9] However, although a maternal aunt and cousin, Jessica and Trudeau,[10] gave signs of having done so, the blond giant had not inherited the very unsavoury character and behaviour of this ancestor.

1. One occasion is recorded in: *The South Will Rise Again*.

2. The incident is described in: *Beguinage*.

3. "Floating Outfit": a group of four to six cowhands employed by a large ranch to work the more distant sections of its range. Taking food in a chuckwagon, or "greasy sack" on the back of a mule, depending upon the expected length of their absence, they would be away from the ranch house for several days at a time. For this reason, they were selected from the most competent and trustworthy members of the crew. Due to the prominence of General Hardin in the affairs of Texas, which his incapacitating injury did not diminish apart from restricting his personal participation, the floating outfit of the OD Connected ranch were frequently sent to assist such of his friends who found themselves in difficulties or endangered.

4. "Right bower": colloquial name for a second in command, deriving from the title of the next to highest trump card in the game of euchre.

5. Details of some of Miss Martha "Calamity Jane" Canary's adventures are recorded in the Calamity Jane series. Her main meetings with Mark Counter are described in: *Part One, "The Bounty On Bell Starr's Scalp"*, *Troubled Range; Part One, "Better Than Calamity"*, *The Wildcats; The Bad Bunch; The Fortune Hunters and Guns In The Night*. She also makes a "guest" appearance in, *Part Two, "A Wife For Dusty Fog"*, *The Small Texan*.

6. How Mark Counter's romance with Belle Starr commenced, progressed and ended is recorded in: *Part One, "The Bounty On Belle Starr's Scalp"*, *Troubled Range*, its "expansion", *Calamity, Mark And Belle; Rangeland Hercules; Part Two, "We Hang Horse Thieves High"*, *J.T.'s Hundredth; The Bad Bunch, The Gentle Giant, Part Four, "A Lady Known As Belle"*, *The Hard Riders* and *Guns In The Night*.

6a. Belle "stars"—no pun intended—in, *Wanted! Belle Starr* and makes "guest" appearances in: *Hell In The Palo Duro; Go Back To Hell; The Quest For Bowie's Blade* and *Part Six, "Mrs. Wild Bill"*, *J.T.'s Ladies*.

6b. We have occasionally been asked why it is that Belle Starr we describe is so much different from the photographs which appear in various books. The researches of fictionist genealogist, Philip José Farmer—author of, among numerous other works, the excellent *Tarzan Alive, A Definitive Biography Of Lord Greystoke* and *Doc Savage, His Apocalyptic Life*— have established that the "Belle Starr" in our books is not the same person as another, equally famous, bearer of the name. However, Andrew

Mark "Big Andy" Counter and Alvin Dustine "Cap" Fog have asked that we and Mr. Farmer keep her true identity a secret and we intend to do so.

7. The three prominent descendants, for whom we have the honour to be biographer—Big Andy, as his name implies, qualifies as possessing the physical qualities, but declines publication of any of his adventures—are:

7a. Ranse Andrew Smith; grandson, formerly a sergeant of Company "Z", Texas Rangers, who makes his first appearance in: *The Justice of Company "Z"*.

7b. Bradford Mark "Brad" Counter; great grandson, serving as a deputy sheriff in Rockabye County, Texas. His career as a peace officer is recorded in the Rockabye County series which also cover various aspects of present day law enforcement.

7c. James Allenvale "Bunduki" Gunn; great grandson, formerly chief warden of the Ambagasali Wild Life Reserve, East Africa, details of whose career can be found in: *Part Twelve, "The Mchawi's Curse", J.T.'s Hundredth* and the Bunduki series. He also makes a "guest" appearance in, *Part Two, "Death to Simba Nyeuse", J.T.'s Ladies*.

8. See: *Ivanhoe*, by Sir Walter Scott.

9. "*Cave Adsum*": roughly translated, "Beware, I Am Here!"

10. Jessica and Trudeau Front de Boeuf appear in: *Cut One, They All Bleed*.

Appendix Three

Raven Head, only daughter of Chief Long Walker, war leader of the *Pehnane*—Wasp, Quick Stinger, or Raider—Comanche's Dog Soldier lodge and his French Creole *pairaivo*,[1] married an Irish-Kentuckian adventurer, Sam Ysabel, but died giving birth to their first child. Baptized "Loncey Dalton" Ysabel, the boy was raised after the fashion of the *Nemenuh*.[2] With his father away much of the time on the family's combined business of mustanging—catching and breaking wild horses—[3] and smuggling, his education had largely been left in the hands of his maternal grandfather.[4] From Long Walker, he had learned all those things a Comanche warrior must know: how to ride the wildest, freshly caught mustang, or make a trained animal subservient to his will when "raiding"—a polite name for the favourite pastime of the male *Nemenuh*, stealing horses—to follow the faintest tracks and just as effectively conceal signs of his own passing;[5] to locate hidden enemies, or keep out of sight himself when the need arose; to move in silence through the thickest cover and on the darkest nights; to know the ways of wild creatures and, in some

169

cases, imitate their calls so that others of their kind might be fooled.[6]

The boy had proved an excellent pupil in all the subjects. He had inherited his father's Kentuckian rifle shooting skill and, while not *real* fast on the draw—taking slightly over a second to bring out and fire his weapon, whereas a top hand could practically half that time—he performed passably with his Colt Second Model of 1848 Dragoon revolver. He had won his *Pehnane* "man-name", *Cuchilo*, Spanish for "Knife," by his exceptional skill in wielding one. It was claimed by those who were best qualified to judge that he could equal the alleged designer in performing with the massive and special type of blade which bore Colonel James Bowie's name.[7]

Joining his father on smuggling expeditions along the Rio Grande, the boy had become known to Mexicans of the border country as *Cabrito*; a name which arose out of hearing white men referring to him as the "Ysabel Kid" and was spoken *very* respectfully in such a context. Smuggling was not an occupation to attract mild-mannered pacifists, but even the roughest and toughest of the bloody border's brood had come to acknowledge it did not pay to rile up Big Sam Ysabel's son. The education received by the Kid had not been calculated to develop any over-inflated belief in the sanctity of human life. When crossed, he dealt with the situation like a *Pehnane* Dog Soldier—to which war lodge of savage and most efficient warriors he had earned initiation—swiftly and in an effectively deadly manner.

During the War Between The States, the Kid and his father had commenced by riding as scouts for Colonel John Singleton "the Grey Ghost" Mosby. Later, their specialized knowledge and talents were converted to having them collect and deliver to the Confederate States' authorities in Texas supplies which had been purchased in Mexico, or run through the blockade by the United States' Navy into Matamoros. It was hard and dangerous work, but never more so than on the two occasions they had become involved in missions with Belle "the Rebel Spy" Boyd.[8]

Soon after the War had ended, Sam Ysabel was murdered. While hunting for the killers, the Kid had met Dusty Fog and Mark Counter. When the assignment upon which they were engaged came to its successful conclusion, learning that the Kid no longer wished to go on either smuggling or mustanging, the small Texan had offered him employment at the OD Connected ranch. It had been in the capacity of scout rather than ordinary cowhand that he was required and his talents were frequently of the greatest use as a member of the floating outfit.

The acceptance of the job by the Kid had been of great benefit all round. The ranch had obtained the services of an extremely capable and efficient man. Dusty acquired a loyal friend who was ready to stick by him through any kind of peril. For his part, the Kid was turned from a life of petty crime—with the ever present danger of having his activities develop into serious law breaking—and became a useful member of society. Peace officers and honest citizens might have found cause to feel thankful for that. His *Nemenuh* upbringing would have made him a terrible and murderous outlaw if he had been driven to a life of crime.

Obtaining his first repeating rifle—a Winchester Model of 1866, nicknamed the "Old Yellowboy" because of its brass frame, although first known as the "New, Improved Henry"—while in Mexico with Dusty and Mark, the Kid had soon become a master in its use. At the first Cochise County Fair in Arizona, he had won first prize in the rifle shooting contest against stiff opposition and despite circumstances having compelled him to rely upon a weapon which was unfamiliar. The prize was one of the legendary

Winchester Model of 1873 rifles which qualified for the title, "One Of A Thousand".[9]

It was, in part, through the efforts of the Kid that the majority of the Comanche bands had agreed to go on to reservations, following the attempts to ruin the treaty signing ceremony at Fort Sorrel.[10] Without his aid, Dusty could not have brought about the closure of the outlaw town called "Hell".[11] Later, he played a major part in preventing the attempted theft of Morton Lewis' ranch provoking trouble with the Comanches[12] and in dealing with the more serious threat posed by the medicine man, Buffalo Bringer.[13] To help a young man out of difficulties with a gang of confidence tricksters, he teamed up with Belle Starr[14] and, when Calamity Jane went to claim a ranch she had inherited, he accompanied her into as dangerous a situation as either had ever faced.[15]

Remaining at the OD Connected ranch, until he, Dusty and Mark met their deaths in Kenya at the turn of the century, whilst in a big game hunt, his descendants continued to be connected with the Hardin, Fog, Blaze clan and the Counter family.[16]

1. *Pairaivo*: first, or favourite, wife. As in the case of other Comanche terms, this is a phonetic spelling.
2. *Nemenuh*: "The People", the Comanches' name for their nation. Members of other tribes with whom they came into contact called them, frequently with good cause, the Tshaoh, the "Enemy People".
3. A description of the ways in which mustangers operated is given in: *.44 Calibre Man* and *A Horse Called Mogollon*.
4. Told in: *Comanche*.
5. An example of the Kid's ability to conceal his tracks is given in: *Part One, "The Half Breed", The Half Breed*.
6. Two incidents in which the Kid turned his knowledge of wild animals to good use are recorded in: *Old Moccasins On The Trail and Part Three, "A Wolf's A Knowing Critter", J.T.'s Hundredth*.
7. Some researchers claim that the actual designer of the knife was James Bowie's eldest brother, Rezin Pleasant. It was made by the master cutler, James Black, of Arkansas. (A few authorities state it was manufactured by Jesse Cliffe, a white blacksmith employed by the Bowie family on

their plantation in Rapides Parish, Louisiana). As all Black's knives were hand-made, there were variations in their dimensions. The specimen owned by the Ysabel Kid had a blade eleven and a half inches long, two and a half wide and a quarter of an inch thick at the guard. According to W.D. "Bo" Randall of Randall Made Knives, Orlando, Florida—a master cutler and authority on the subject—James Bowie's knife weighed forty-three ounces, having a blade eleven inches long, two and a quarter inches wide and three-eights of an inch thick. His company's Model 12 "Smithsonian" bowie knife—one of which is owned by James Allenvale "Bunduki" Gunn, q.v.—is modelled on it. What happened to James Bowie's knife after his death in the final assault at the siege of the Alamo Mission, San Antonio de Bexar, on March the 6th, 1836, is told in: *Get Urrea* and *The Quest For Bowie's Blade*.

7a. One thing all bowie knives have in common, regardless of dimensions, is a "clip" point. The otherwise unsharpened back of the blade joins and becomes an extension of the cutting edge in a concave arc, whereas a "spear" point is formed by the two sides coming together in symmetrical curves.

8. Told in: *The Bloody Border* and *Back To The Bloody Border* (U.S.A. Berkley edition retitled, *Renegade*).

9. When manufacturing the extremely popular Winchester Model of 1873 rifle, the makers selected all those having barrels found to shoot with exceptional accuracy to be fitted with set triggers and given a special fine finish. Originally, these were inscribed "1 of 1,000", but this was later changed to script, "One Of A Thousand". However, the title was a considerable understatement as only one hundred and thirty-six out of a total production of 720,610 rifles qualified for the distinction. Those of a grade lower were to be designated, "One Of A Hundred", but only seven were so named. The practice was commenced in 1875 and was discontinued three years later because the management decided it was not good policy to suggest different grades of gun were being produced.

10. Told in: *Sidewinder*.

11. Told in: *Hell In The Palo Duro* and *Go Back To Hell*.

12. Told in: *White Indians*.

13. Told in: *Buffalo Are Coming!*

14. Told in: *Part One, "The Poison And The Cure"*, *Wanted! Belle Starr*.

15. Told in: *White Stallion, Red Mare*.

16. A grandson of the Ysabel Kid, Mark Scrapton, served as a member of Company "Z", Texas Rangers, with Alvin Dustine "Cap" Fog and Ranse Andrew Smith during the Prohibition era. On undercover assignments, he frequently adopted an alias used by his grandfather under similar circumstances, "Comanche Blood".

Appendix Four

Left an orphan almost from birth by a Waco Indian raid, from whence came the only name he knew, Waco had been raised as one of a North Texas rancher's large family.[1] Guns had always been a part of his life and his sixteenth birthday had seen him riding with the tough, "wild onion" ranch crew of Clay Allison. Like their employer, the CA hands were notorious for their wild and occasionally dangerous behaviour. Living in the company of such men, all older than himself, he had become quick to take offense and well able, eager even, to prove he could draw his revolvers with lightning speed and shoot very accurately. It had seemed only a matter of time before one shootout too many would see him branded as a killer and fleeing from the law with a price on his head.

Fortunately for Waco and—as was the case with the Ysabel Kid—law abiding citizens, that day did not come!

From the moment Dusty Fog saved the youngster's life, at considerable risk to his own, a change for the better had come.[2] Leaving Allison, with the blessing of the Washita curly wolf, Waco had become a member of the OD Connected ranch's floating outfit. The others of this elite group had treated him like a favourite younger brother and taught him many useful lessons. Mark Counter gave him instruction in bare-handed combat. The Kid showed him how to read tracks and many other tricks of the scout's trade. From a friend who was a professional gambler, Frank Derringer, had come information about the ways of honest and dishonest followers of his chosen field of endeavour. However, it had been from the Rio Hondo gun wizard that the most important advice of all had come. *When*, he already knew *how* to shoot. Dusty had also supplied training which, helped by an inborn flare for deductive reasoning, turned him into a peace officer of exceptional merit.[3] Benefiting from such a wide education, he became noted in law enforcement circles. Having served with Marvin Eldridge "Doc" Leroy[4] as a member of the first Arizona Rangers[5] and as sheriff of Two Forks County, Utah,[6] he was eventually appointed a United States' marshal.[7]

1. How Waco repaid the obligation to his adoptive father is told in: *Waco's Debt*. Alvin Dustine "Cap" Fog informs us that, at his marriage to Elizabeth "Beth" Morrow, Waco used the name of his adoptive family, "Catlan".

2. Told in: *Trigger Fast*.

3. Told in: *The Making Of A Lawman; The Trouble Busters; The Gentle Giant; Part Five, "The Hired Butcher", The Hard Riders; Part Four, "A Tolerable Straight Shooting Gun," The Floating Outfit; The Small Texan* and *The Town Tamers*.

4. Although at the period of this narrative Marvin Eldridge "Doc" Leroy had not yet been able to attain his ambition of following in his father's footsteps by becoming a qualified doctor, he was already very knowledgeable in medical matters. The murder of his parents in a range war caused him to put aside his intended departure to attend a medical school in St. Louis, Missouri. Nevertheless, he took every opportunity to study and improve his practical skills. What was more, while earning his living as a cowhand with the Wedge trail drive crew, as a member of the OD Connected ranch's floating outfit and in the Arizona Rangers, he found many occasions when circumstances required he engaged upon the profession to which he aspired. In fact, due to the number with which he was called upon to deal, he could even now claim to know more about the treatment of gunshot wounds than many a practitioner who could affix the honori-

fic, Doctor of Medicine. There were those he declared his ability to remove bullets was equal to the speed and accuracy with which he could
send them in when the need to do so arose. Like Waco, he had been
taught the tricks of crooked gamblers by an expert and was able to detect,
or even duplicate, cheating methods. How he was finally able to qualify is
told in: *Doc Leroy, M.D.*

5. Told in: *Waco's Badge; Sagebrush Sleuth; Arizona Ranger; Part Six,
"Keep Good Temper Alive", J.T.'s Hundredth* and *Waco Rides In.*
6. Told in: *The Drifter.*
7. Told in: *Hound Dog Man.*

Appendix Five

Throughout the years we have been writing, we have frequently received letters asking for various Western terms, or incidents to which we refer, to be explained in greater detail. While we do not have the slightest objection to receiving such mail and *always* answer, we have found it saves much time-consuming correspondence to include those most often requested in each new title. We ask all our "old hands" who have seen this Appendix to bear with us and remember there are always "new chums" coming along who have not.

1. We strongly suspect that the trend in film and television Westerns made since the mid-1960's to portray all cowhands as long haired, heavily bearded and filthy stems less from the desire of the production companies to create "realism" than because there were so few actors available—particularly to play supporting roles—who were short haired and clean shaven. Another factor was because the "liberal" elements, who were gaining control of the mass entertainment media, seem to obtain some form of ego trip from showing dirty conditions, appearances and habits. On our extensive reference library, we cannot find even a dozen photographs of actual cowhands—as opposed to Army scouts, mountain men or old time gold prospectors—with long hair and bushy beards. In fact, our reading on the subject and conversations with friends in the modern West have led us to the conclusion that the term "long hair" was one of opprobrium in the Ole

West and Prohibition eras just as it still tends to be in cattle raising country today.

2. "Make wolf bait": one term meaning to kill. It derives from the practice in the Old West, when a range was infested by stock destroying predators —not necessarily just wolves, but coyotes, black or grizzly bears—of slaughtering an animal and, having poisoned the carcase, leaving it to be devoured by the carnivores.

3. "Gone to Texas": on the run from the law, generally in the United States at the time when the saying was first brought into usage. Many fugitives from justice entered Texas during the colonization period— which had commenced in the early 1820's, due to the Mexican Government offering land to "Anglos" so they would act as a "buffer state" against marauding Comanche and Kiowa Indians—and continued until annexation as a State of the Union on February the 16th, 1846. Before the latter became a fact, such miscreants had known there was little danger of being arrested and extradited by the local authorities. Therefore, like Kenya during the 1920's until the outbreak of World War II, in spite of the great number of honest, law-abiding and hard-working people who genuinely wished to make their homes there, Texas during the days prior to independence being gained from Mexican domination acquired a reputation for being "a place in the sun for shady people".

4. Mason-Dixon line, also erroneously called the "Mason-Dixie" line. The boundary between Pennsylvania and Maryland, as surveyed in 1763–67 by the Englishmen, Charles Mason and Jeremiah Dixon. It became known as the dividing line separating the Southern "Slave" and Northern "Free" States.

5. New England: the North East section of the United States, including Massachusetts, New Hampshire, Maine, Vermont, Connecticut and Rhode Island, which was first settled primarily by people from the British Isles.

6. "Light a shuck": cowhands' term for leaving hurriedly. It derives from the habit in night camps of roundups and trail drives of supplying "shucks"—dried corn cobs—to be lit and used for illumination by anybody who had to leave the camp-fire and walk in the darkness. As the "shuck" burned away very quickly, a person needed to hurry if wanting to benefit from the light.

7. Although Americans in general used the word "cinch", derived from the Spanish, "cincha", to describe the short band made from coarsely woven horsehair, canvas, or cordage and terminated at each end with a metal ring which—together with the latigo—is used to fasten the saddle on the back of a horse, because of its Spanish connotations, Texans employ the term "girth", usually pronouncing it, "girt". As cowhands of the Lone Star State fastened the end of the lariat to the saddlehorn when roping half wild longhorn cattle, or free-ranging mustangs, instead of using a "dally" which could be slipped free almost instantaneously in an emergency, their rigs had double girths.

8. The sharp toes and high heels of the boots worn by cowhands were purely functional. The former could find and enter, or be slipped from, a stirrup iron very quickly in an emergency. Not only did the latter offer a firmer grip in the stirrups, they could be spiked into the ground to supply extra holding power when roping on foot.

9. "Chaps"; leather overalls worn by American cowhands as protection for the legs. The word, pronounced "shaps", is an abbreviation of the Spanish, chaperejos (chaparreras), meaning "leather breeches". Contrary to what is shown in many Western movies, no cowhand kept on his chaps when they were not required for their intended use. Even if he arrived in town with them on, he would remove and either hang them from his saddlehorn or leave them behind the bar of his favourite saloon for safe keeping for the duration of his visit.

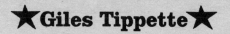